MISTAKEN IDENTITY

MINDY BURBIDGE STRUNK

Other Books by Mindy Burbidge Strunk

An American in Duke's Clothing

Reforming the Gambler

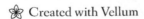 Created with Vellum

ACKNOWLEDGMENTS

A big thanks to Rob Dinsdale and my friends at Chick-Fil-A for allowing me to hang out in their dining room, sometimes when they were not even open, so I could write in quiet.

To Jenny Proctor, my fabulous editor who helps me with my comma addiction and gives great insight when I have used all of mine up.

For my great writers' group: Dickens, Heyer, Bronte and Austen! I didn't know what I was missing before I found you guys. Writing this book series with you has been something I will always treasure.

To Kim Ball and Patti Knowlton for beta reading, sometimes at break neck speed. You guys are the best!

And last and most importantly, for my boys. Thanks for not complaining when you were out of clean clothes or got pizza for dinner...again, while I edited for what seemed like the millionth time. Especially to Christopher for supporting and helping me push through when it just felt too hard. You are my greatest cheer-leader! I love you guys!

PROLOGUE

Unrequited Love

Jessica Standish sat next to her aunt watching the dancers swish about the dance floor. Her eyes followed one particular couple. Lord Ian Pinkerton led Miss Parker through the steps of a cotillion. They both smiled prettily at each other as she passed in front of him. Jes squinted and a frown pulled down the corner of her lips.

Her eyes darted away from the seemingly happy couple, landing on the determined face of Mr. Westoff. His eyes set upon her and his pace quickened.

Jes looked toward her aunt, hoping she would save her from dancing with a man known among society to be a complete bore. Even his gait was starched and stiff. His face wore a perpetual frown.

"May I have this dance?" Mr. Westoff bowed before her. She

stood reluctantly when she realized her aunt would be of no assistance.

With a polite curtsy, she glanced quickly over Mr. Westoff's shoulder as she rose. Lord Ian bowed over Miss Jenkin's hand and Jes knew he would not be asking her for this dance. It seemed Mr. Westoff was to be her partner. She placed a false smile on her face. "Of course, Mr. Westoff. It would be my pleasure."

Jes danced the Scottish Reel from memory, hardly noticing the steps she took. She smiled at the appropriate times, hoping to convince her partner she was paying him mind, but whenever she passed behind him or out of his view, her eyes searched out Lord Ian.

Why do I do this to myself? She thought.

It was out of habit rather than any belief Lord Ian would take notice of her. After all, it was the last ball of the season, and he had yet to even glance in her direction.

The dance ended and she curtsied again as Mr. Westoff kissed her gloved hand, before relinquishing her to the care of her aunt, Lady Mayfield.

"You may have fooled that dolt, but do not think you fooled me." Aunt Lydia fluttered her fan rapidly. "I saw the way you kept seeking him out. I have warned you about setting your sights on that gentleman, Jessica. He is a complete rake and would destroy your tenuous status within the ton."

"It is not as if anything will come of it. He has never even looked in my direction." Jes could not hide the regret lacing her words as her eyes sought him out again.

Lord Ian stood across the room, conversing with a young woman Jes did not know. He picked up a loose tendril of hair and tucked it intimately behind the lady's ear.

Another sigh escaped Jes's lips.

Lord Ian straightened, his gaze darting around the room. As it came to the side where Jes sat with her aunt, she dropped her gaze to her hands. Slowly bringing her eyes up, she watched him through her lashes.

Her heart pounded as she saw him walking toward her. Just when she thought it might burst from her chest, he stopped in front of Aunt Lydia.

"Lady Mayfield." Lord Ian bowed.

He was so elegant. Jes dared not look directly at him, for fear her thoughts would be evident in her gaze.

"I do not believe I have had the pleasure of being introduced to your..." He paused.

"Niece." Aunt Lydia provided. She gave him a disdainful look —one that would quell any other gentleman. "Lord Ian, may I introduce Miss Jessica Standish. Her mother, Lady Rachel Standish is my sister."

Before Jes could process and truly enjoy what was happening, she found herself being led to the dance floor on the arm of Lord Ian, where they completed the square with Mr. Beauchamp and Miss Jennings. For the first time this season, Jes found it impossible to look away from her partner. He was everything she had imagined: charming, witty, beautiful. In that moment, she knew no other man would ever come close to measuring up.

CURSES AND LIES

"*B*loo..." Conrad Pinkerton, the Marquess of Kendal, cursed to himself. He reined in his horse at the sight of several carriages lining the drive of the massive house. If he waited his turn in line, he would surely be caught in the approaching downpour, just visible in the distance. He moved his horse to the side, the stables his destination, passing ladies dressed in all their finery as they exited their carriages. Servants followed behind, loaded down with trunks and boxes of varying sizes. Probably filled with bonnets of great extravagance and even less taste.

Conrad snorted. He had no idea how Ian had convinced him to agree to this absurd plan. Demonic possession seemed the only explanation for what he was about to do. He hated society and a house party was one of the worst manifestations of it. Every mama able to finagle an invitation would be here to peddle her daughter before the highest ranking peer. It was beyond his understanding of why his brother willingly submitted himself to this tabby gathering. Under normal circumstances, Conrad would never attend such an event, yet here he was.

He handed off his mount to a stable boy.

Moving quickly in front of the ladies currently being helped from their carriage, Conrad muttered another curse. A sharp intake of breath drew his gaze to a young woman waiting for the rest of her party. She looked at him with wide eyes.

Conrad dipped his head in apology and mounted the curved stairs, joining the other guests there.

An old hunched butler stood just inside the open doorway, gesturing him inside. Conrad presented his card, or rather, Ian's.

"Lord Ian Pinkerton, welcome to Somerstone." The old man bowed so deeply, Conrad was afraid he may never be able to right himself again. Much to his relief, the man returned to his previous hunched position before reaching behind Conrad and taking the card of the group behind him.

A slim, dark-haired lady approached with a bright smile. She was not a doe-eyed debutante, but neither did she look to be on the shelf. She, or rather her family, must have money problems, Conrad thought with a small amount of sympathy.

"Ah, Lord Ian. I am Miss Graystock, the Countess's companion. Lady Du'Brevan has been waiting for you. Please, follow me. She wanted to speak with you directly."

Conrad sighed internally, for Ian would never make such a sound out loud. Unless it was a matter of grave concern, such as a mis-tied cravat or a waistcoat of last year's fashion. Having committed himself the moment he walked through the door, Conrad pasted a smile upon his face, one he hoped conveyed a mixture of fecklessness and charm. The action proved more difficult than he had assumed. He loathed the role he must play, but he *had* agreed. Switching places was something they had done throughout childhood. Then it was a perk of being identical twins. Now the joke was stale and juvenile. Straightening Ian's canary yellow waistcoat and checking that his hair was parted on the correct side, Conrad squared his shoulders and followed the woman through a hall with dozens of pillars supporting the upper floor. At the stairs, the lady waited for him to ascend first.

So, she has been trained to be a lady, then. His earlier suspicions were supported. At the top of the stairs, he again followed Miss Graystock down a sort of hallway, although it went through several rooms along the way. Conrad looked around, without openly gawking. Ian had been a guest of the Countess on several occasions. It would surely give Conrad away if he seemed overly interested in the grand home.

Conrad himself had only met the Countess Du'Breven on a few occasions in London. He did not know her well, but he did know her to be a busybody who, on occasion, could prove amusing. Perhaps the next few days would not be horrendous, after all.

He followed Miss Graystock into a library of sorts, although its offering was sparse compared to many, including his own. From the expansiveness of the house, Conrad guessed it was more likely a personal sitting room of the Countess. The bookshelves only covered the lower half of the walls, the upper portion was covered in a rich red wallpaper. Windows spread throughout the room gave it a bright, welcoming warmth. The lady herself was seated at a desk, a quill in hand. She looked up at their entrance. Abandoning her parchment, she stood to greet them.

Miss Graystock curtsied. "I will see to the other guests unless you need me for something else, my lady?"

The Countess waved her away and Miss Graystock closed the door behind her. Conrad envied the woman's quick exit.

The old woman's shoulders relaxed a fraction as she smiled. "Ian, it is so good to see you."

"I can assure you, my lady, the pleasure is all mine." Had he used enough affection in his tone? Did his smile appear appropriately friendly? He should have paid more attention to Ian in social gatherings. Although, he tried to avoid doing both. Conrad took a calming breath. How had he thought this charade was going to work?

The Countess clasped his hands in hers, unabashedly looking him over. The scrutiny was unnerving. Conrad unconsciously took a step back, his smile dropping slightly, only to have the Countess take two steps forward, closing the gap. Her eyes narrowed slightly as she continued her perusal. Stopping at his face, her head tilting to one side. *I can't believe it. I have been here less than five minutes and the lady has already ferreted out the secret.*

"You seem different, Ian. I can't quite put my finger on it, but there is definitely something amiss."

Conrad pushed his hair out of his eyes determining to have his valet trim it tonight. Forcing a chuckle that came out sounding slightly crazed, he stammered. "I...I do not know what you mean. Perhaps my hair is longer than usual, but..." He raised a brow, hoping he could distract her until he could make an escape to his rooms. "You, on the other hand, have not changed a bit. How do you do it, my lady?" *I have two whole days of this?* He was beginning to think his best course of action was to keep to his rooms. Or rather to any room where the Countess was not.

She released his hands and rapped him lightly against the upper arm. "I can see you have not changed in totality. You are still quite the charmer."

Conrad gave an inward grimace at the description. It inferred such low character. He did not understand how his brother could not only endure such a title but seemingly embrace it. "I was told you wished to see me upon my arrival." He winced slightly at the gruff tone of his voice. Softening it, he asked, "How may I be of service?"

Her head tilted again, an appraising look entering her eyes.

Moving back to her desk, she picked up the feather, tapping it against her chin. "I was hoping you had convinced your brother to accompany you on this visit. But seeing you are alone, I am guessing he was otherwise engaged?" There was a touch of challenge in her voice.

"My dear Countess, if I did not know better, I would think you were using me for my connections to the Marquess of Kendal." He gave a dramatic sigh, followed by a wink. He had seen Ian wink hundreds of times at as many ladies. It always ended with the same response —tittering and blushing. The Countess, however, neither blushed nor tittered, which squelched Conrad's earlier confidence. "It is good I know better," he quickly amended. "I did present him with your invitation, but as always, he declined. I cannot fathom why you desire his presence. Everyone knows he is a bore and most disagreeable." Conrad had heard himself described in these terms many times over the years. Along with contrary, surly, and disobliging. He had begun to wear the descriptions as a badge of honor.

The Countess waved away his words. "On the few occasions I have met Lord Kendal, I found him reserved, but not entirely unpleasant." A puzzled expression crossed her face before she turned her back and took up her seat. "Very well. I shall see you at dinner."

Not waiting for her to change her mind, Conrad bowed in her direction and made his way out of the room. He was almost to the door when her words stopped him. "Lord Kendal?"

Conrad turned. "Yes, my la...?" What had she just called him? Was it just a mistake on her part? He chanced a look in her direction, but her head was still down, her feather moving furiously back and forth.

"You will have to try harder if you are to persuade anyone here that you are, indeed, Lord Ian. Granted, I am more observant than most, but there are several attending who boast quite an intimate acquaintance with your brother. Namely Lord Anthony and Mr. Beauchamp."

Conrad's back stiffened at the mention of Ian's school chums. They were three men of the same ilk.

She finally looked up from her work. "I am surprised either of you believed you could fool me." There was a touch of arrogance in her voice.

Conrad shrugged. "I tried to tell Ian this would never work, but he was insistent. His visit with Miss Simmons overlapped by a few days. He was afraid of offending you."

"Thinking me a dimwit is what I find offensive." The terseness of her voice told Conrad she was not happy with their plan. Hope blossomed in him. Was she so offended she would ask him to leave?

She stood, moving in his direction. "I find I am intrigued with the possible outcomes of this little charade, not to mention honored to have the Marquess of Kendal at my little house party." She quirked a brow, her lips pursed. "Tell me, when is your brother expected?"

Conrad's shoulders dropped and he let out a heavy breath. Not soon enough. "Tomorrow next, my lady."

She clasped her hands, a wicked smile on her face. "Then we shall need to have our fun quickly, my lord."

Conrad shook his head. "Now that you are aware of this ruse, I shall be on my way."

The Countess cackled. "Oh, no. You started this little game, Lord Kendal and you will see it though. At least until your brother turns up." Her brows raised in challenge. "And then perhaps, you could arrive again...as yourself."

Conrad smiled tightly at her as he gave a curt nod, barely stifling his groan.

"TELL me again how you procured this invitation, Mama?" Jes stared out the rain-streaked carriage window at the vast home visible between the birch trees lining the drive. The darkness of the storm clouds overhead merely made the expansive house look ominous.

"Do not act so astonished, Jes. We may be paupers now, but there was a time when all the grand homes in England were open to me. I was even dear friends with the daughter of the Countess Du'Brevan."

Jes turned sympathetic eyes to her mother. "We are not paupers, Mama." Not that it had mattered when they did have money. "Though, it still does not explain the invitation. Our less than winning reputation among society was made very clear during my last season." She knew her words were harsh, but none the less true.

"Come now, Jes." There was a hint of aggravation in Lady Rachel's voice. "Wipe that suspicion from your face. I did nothing dishonest. I simply made contact with an old acquaintance."

With each turn of the wheels, Jes felt her unease increase. These were not her friends. There were bound to be people in attendance she met while in London. They had not wanted her friendship then, why should they want it now? "Perhaps we could return to Aunt Lydia's. There is bound to be a cottage nearby we could let with the money we have left."

Her mother looked out the window, conveniently avoiding eye contact. "As to the remaining money, I am afraid the bulk of it is gone." At Jes's sharp intake of breath, her mother turned back to her. "We could not arrive here in a mail coach wearing rags, now could we? It was necessary to use the remainder of the money to..."

Her mother paused. "Put our best foot forward. This is precisely the type of event that could change your life."

Jes shook her head. "But Mama, you said Aunt Lydia paid for all of this." She lifted the fabric of her new traveling dress.

Her mother shrugged. "I knew you would dig in your heels if I told you where the money was coming from. It is a risk, I know. But the risk I believe is necessary."

"Do you not remember London? If I could not secure a match there, among dozens of eligible men, what makes you believe I would make one here?" Her voice dropped to nearly a whisper. "I will be seen as a fortune hunter." She turned toward the window, resting her forehead against the pane. A sigh of frustration puffed out her lips. How could her mother have done such a thing? This irrational woman was not the mother Jes knew. She whispered her newest fear into her hands. "It will all come to naught and we will be left with nothing."

Her mother placed a hand on her back, rubbing small circles, taking Jes back to her childhood. "It is not for me I am doing this. It is for you. I want you to be happy and well settled."

Lifting her head from the glass, Jes turned. "And I can only be well settled and happy with a gentleman of large fortune? It was not the life you chose for yourself."

Lady Rachel's head dropped to the side. "I loved your father and we had a good life, but that does not mean there were not difficult times. I am trying to help you avoid that."

Jes turned back to the window, her eyes widening as Somerstone came into clear view. "Everyone has difficulties, Mama. Even the rich and titled. You should know that as well as anyone."

The carriage moved forward, stopping in front of the curved steps. Jes moved to the edge of the seat, anticipating the footman opening the door. She was not, however, anticipating his very handsome face. He smiled, making her face warm slightly. Lady

Rachel cleared her throat, moving Jes's feet just a little faster. Once they were both on the ground, he handed them off to another footman.

Jes entered the house, stopping in the entryway. Her mind could not process the opulence of the house. Lady Rachel touched her arm, leaning in so only Jes could hear. "It is amazing, is it not?"

Nodding, Jes whispered back. "Have you never been here before?"

Lady Rachel shook her head. "No, my associations with the Du'Brevens was in London. Although, I did attend a house party at their estate in Kent one summer."

They followed the footman through a room filled with pillars and up one side of the rounded staircase. As they reached the first landing, movement on the floor above drew Jes's notice. She looked up. Her heart quickened and her breath caught in her throat. It could not be. *He* was here. She felt the wetness of her palms beneath her gloves. It had been nearly two years since she saw him last. In point of fact, she had given up the hope she would ever see him again. But here he was.

2

BOORISH DINNER PARTNERS

*C*onrad stood against the wall of the sitting room, watching the guests milling about and waiting for dinner to be served. Mothers and daughters moved from group to group, tittering and laughing at each one, as if every person in attendance was particularly witty. Conrad's chin lifted and his lip curled in irritation. This display was society at its worst. He could see the calculation in the eyes of every mother—weighing each gentleman's character by the size of his fortune and the title he held. Surely, a marquess would be deemed a man of great character. This was one of the few times Conrad was glad everyone here believed him to be Ian.

While Ian was charming and handsome enough that every young lady wished to be seen on his arm, very few fathers considered him a suitable prospect for their daughters. Such was the lot of a second son—even if it were by only four minutes. Although, being the second son was not the only thing keeping Ian from the daughters of the beau monde. The rumors of his gambling troubles were beginning to circulate.

Hopes of an agreement between Ian and Miss Simmons was the only reason Conrad had agreed to this charade. If subjecting himself to this...pedantic display would lead Ian to settle down with a respectable young lady of large fortune, Conrad was willing to sacrifice.

"What are you scowling about?" Lord Anthony stood at his side. "It makes you look like your brother."

Conrad shrugged, placing the lazy smile he had been practicing on his lips. "Funny. I was just thinking of my brother."

Lord Anthony leaned back against the wall. "What did his greatness, the Marquess of Kendal do now?"

Conrad held back a smile. He knew his brother and his friends spoke less than flatteringly about him. "Same as always. He will not continue to pay my debts if I do not come about."

Lord Anthony laughed. "Some things never change. His Highness is always good for a lecture. Gratefully, he will never actually carry out his threats." Something drew Lord Anthony's attention away. "Excuse me, Ian. I need to speak with someone."

Conrad scowled. They believed he would never follow through, did they? He ground his teeth together as his gaze made another circuit about the room. A young lady entered on the far side. She was not overly beautiful, yet Conrad could not seem to take his eyes off her. A small group opposite him seemed to be her intended destination, however after a quick perusal, her eyes lit and she changed her course, heading instead towards him.

She stepped up to him, dipping a slight curtsy. "Lord Ian. It is good to see you again."

Placing what he hoped looked like an indolent smile on his face, he nodded. "I quite agree, but remind me, when did we last see each other? It seems to be ages ago."

She smiled as if she knew he was searching for information. "It was in London...at the Medford's ball, the season last."

"Ah, yes. The Medford's ball." He knew the Medfords. They were a decent sort of people, but not the upper tier by any stretch of the imagination. It rather surprised him Ian would attend such an affair.

"And how have you been since last we met?" she asked.

It was most unlike Ian to associate with a woman such as this, for she did not possess the beauty of most of Ian's conquests. She either came from great wealth or...Conrad did not want to think on the other reasons Ian might have shown interest in this young lady. He shook his head at his unfavorable thoughts of his brother. What had happened to their friendship over the last several years?

The woman looked at him curiously. Perhaps it would be best if he did not take so long to answer questions. "I am doing well. I thank you for inquiring." She looked around the room. No doubt she was searching for better company. He wished he knew her name, not that it would help this fledgling conversation.

He cleared his throat, bringing her attention back. "Are you here with your mother or..." He groaned inwardly. What was he prattling on about? Staring at a wall would be of more interest than this conversation. How did Ian do it? He always made conversation look so effortless. Conrad tried for a lighter tone.

The young lady gave a polite smile, her gaze not fully connecting with his. "Yes, my mother accompanied me. In fact, here she comes now." Her head nodded in the opposite direction.

A beautiful woman walked regally towards them. He looked back at the young lady next to him, noting the resemblance. The mother was striking, while the daughter was more... pretty. Though the girl's dark brown eyes did play to her advantage, bringing out the pink in her cheeks. The mother reached them, standing at her daughter's side. "Who do we have here, Jes? I do not believe I have made the gentleman's acquaintance."

Jes? That did him very little good in his current situation. It was not as if he could call the young lady by her Christian name, but for now, it was better than no name at all. Jes placed a hand on her mother's arm. "Lady Rachel Standish, may I introduce Lord Ian Pinkerton. Lord Ian and I meet in London when I was there with Aunt Lydia."

Lady Rachel curtsied. "My lord."

Conrad bowed, kissing the lady's hand. Ah, finally. He had a name, but was she Lady Jes or Miss Standish? "It is a pleasure to meet you Lady Rachel. You have a very charming daughter." The young lady pinked slightly at the compliment. The color served to brighten her already alluring eyes. A thrill tingled in his chest.

Just then, the Countess sidled up beside him. "Ah, Lord Ian." She emphasized his name. If the woman continued this way, everyone would know something was amiss. "I see you have met Lady Rachel and her daughter, Miss Jessica Standish."

Conrad nodded in Miss Standish's direction. *Finally, her name.* "It would be hard to miss someone as lovely as Miss Standish." The blush deepened and Conrad found it difficult to swallow. *Perhaps this is why Ian acts as he does.* "Although, Miss Standish and I already had the pleasure of meeting...in London." He stumbled over the explanation. "At the Medford's ball." He added lamely. How could someone of his status be so bad at something as simple as speaking? Any feelings of success or delight vanished. Conrad took a deep breath. Ian would never stammer like a schoolboy.

Lady Du'Breven coughed, although it sounded more like a laugh. "Is that so, Lord Ian?" There was that tone again.

Miss Standish nodded her head vigorously. She had obviously mistaken the Countess's odd reaction to mean their story was not believable. Anger surged through him. This was all a jest, a diversion to the old woman. It was another reason Conrad hated society. He abhorred all the games they played. He chagrined slightly, as he realized he was playing a game as surely as anyone here.

The Countess patted Miss Standish on the arm as if to reassure her. Turning to Lady Rachel, she continued. "Lord Ian is the brother of the Marquess of Kendal."

Lady Rachel smiled tightly, the warmth disappearing from her gaze. "I was acquainted with your mother," she said to Conrad. "She and my sister had their come outs together. She was a very... refined lady."

Conrad felt his heart tug at the mention of his mother, momentarily forgetting those around him. "Yes, she was. Were you close friends?"

The smile dropped from Lady Rachel's mouth. "Yes, we *were*."

Conrad frowned slightly. If they had been friends, why the frown?

The Countess coughed again, placing her hand on Lady Rachel's. "Come, my dear. I seem to have a tickle in my throat. Perhaps we can find something to assuage it until dinner is served." The two women moved away, leaving Miss Standish behind.

Her gaze continued to move around the room. Conrad was sure she was anxious to find someone else to converse with. Fiend seize it, he wasn't good at being his brother. How could it be so difficult to play an idiot? Ian made it all look so simple—a smile here, a wink there. Yet, Conrad was having difficulty with a simple conversation. He needed to think of something to make him smile naturally and genuinely. A smile broke free as thoughts of punishing Ian when this all was over rolled through his mind.

Miss Standish turned back towards him. "Is your brother attending? I have not had the pleasure of an introduction. You never mentioned your brother when we were in London."

It was not surprising Ian had never mentioned a brother to her.

Conrad leaned in as if they were conspirators. "You most likely will never be introduced." She frowned and Conrad realized how the statement must have sounded. He hurried to correct himself. "Only because he abhors these types of events and rejects every invitation. Unless you travel to his estate in Westmorland, it is doubtful the opportunity will present itself."

Her face turned crimson and not for a good reason this time. "I did not know. My apologies for making such an assumption." She pulled away slightly, seemingly ill at ease with their close proximity.

He winked. It felt foreign and odd. "There is no need to apologize. I am sure it is for the best. He is terribly tedious and no fun at all."

Miss Standish bit her lower lip before she responded. "I cannot believe it. I have yet to meet anyone with nothing of interest to say. I am sure your brother is not so very different." She looked off at something on the other side of the room. "It is too bad I shall not have the opportunity to find out for myself."

The butler entered and announced dinner. Miss Standish offered a small curtsy before hurrying to join her mother as the group began to order themselves for the move into the dining room. Conrad watched her leave and felt...perplexed. Who was this intriguing woman?

Jes and her mother were seated about halfway down the dining table, separated only by a gentleman. Apparently, her mother's title still held some clout, in this household, at least. Or, perhaps not. Jes looked up and down the table, taking note of where others were seated. Lord Ian was seated next to the Countess. Curious, she thought. While he was a lord, it was only a courtesy title, given to all sons of a marquess. Many in attendance boasted greater status than that of a younger son. But then, the Countess was quite known for ignoring social protocol.

"Ah, Miss Standish. I see we have been placed next to each other." Lord Bloomsbury patted at his sweat-dotted forehead with his handkerchief.

She feigned a smile. "You have a very good memory, Lord Bloomsbury. Many gentlemen would not have remembered my name among this crush." The baron flopped the long strands of hair he used to cover his balding crown, back into place. "Mother always says manners require a good memory."

Jes placed a finger to her mouth, trying to hide her amusement. An army of footmen entered, bringing dishes to the table. The chatter of voices quieted, only to be replaced by the clattering of dishes. Covers were removed and the food dished onto the plates. Lord Bloomsbury turned his attention to Miss Burton across the table. The gentleman on Jes's other side—apparently, she had poor manners, for she had forgotten his name—was engrossed in conversation with Lord and Lady Wilmington.

Jes began eating, lost in her own thoughts. Her eyes moved of their own volition down the table to Lord Ian. He seemed much changed since last she saw him. Granted, she had only danced with him once, but she had observed him. More than was acceptable, according to Aunt Lydia. He was acting more reserved and withdrawn than he had in London. When he looked up and their gazes locked, she realized she was staring. Her face heated. She ducked her head and focused on the plate in front of her.

"Do you not agree, Miss Standish?" Lord Bloomsbury looked at her with an expectant gaze.

Jes swallowed her bite, taking in the many eyes turned to her. "I'm sorry, I did not hear the question."

"I was explaining to Miss Barton that there is far too much riffraff imposing on the ranks of society."

Confusion wrinkled Jes's brow. "I am afraid I do not understand what you are speaking of. I was not a party to your earlier conversation."

The baron rose a disdainful brow. "Mother and I were talking of this just the other day. It seems the ton is being overrun by upstarts, the offspring of simple tradesmen or merchants, who feel they are of the same social importance...just because they have made some blunt along the way." He sniffed in indignation, before continuing. "Can you imagine the state of society in only a handful of years if we continue to let this happen? It is not to be borne."

Jes closed her slack mouth tightly. She was not sure if he was accusing her personally or an entire class of people generally. What was she to say? If she agreed with him, she would be a hypocrite, having been exactly that her last season. But if she disagreed and made her station known, she and her mother would do just as well to pack their bags and return to Durham.

"Well?" A nasally female voice down the table barked sharply. "My son asked you a question, miss. Are your manners so neglected you do not offer a response?" The older woman, with lips pursed, stared down her pointed nose at Jes.

Jes's head snapped back in surprise. "I am sorry. I did not have any opinion to add, therefore I felt it better to remain silent."

Lady Bloomsbury harrumphed. "The youth of today are woefully uneducated. And their manners..."

Jes's pride reared up at the slight. Straightening her back, she looked pointedly at the old woman. "Your son seems to have covered the subject to his satisfaction." The table was silent, every eye riveted on her and the Baroness. "My mother says, if I cannot say anything nice, I should not say anything at all. Perhaps I should stop speaking now."

Jes heard a few intakes of breath and several gasps. The Countess let out a loud cackle from the end of the table, while the Baroness sat with her mouth gaping open and her eyes wide with shock. "Well, of all the...."

Before the woman could finish the insult Jes knew would follow, she turned to the gentleman on her other side. She scrunched up her brow, still unable to recall his name, and asked, "Have you tasted the duckling? I believe I have never tasted anything it's equal." Smiling an innocent smile, she stuck a forkful of meat into her mouth. She paid little attention to what the man said. He seemed content to make inconsequential, small talk.

As the occupants of the dining room resumed their conversations, Jes could feel the stares at the back of her head. Part of her wanted to turn and see who it was, but another part of her was suddenly too tired. Too tired of putting on a show. Too tired of caring about society's opinion of her and her family. Too tired of dealing with mean, arrogant people. If not for the fear of what would be said about her mother, Jes would have left the table right then. She did not care what people said of her, but her mother did not deserve to be censured because of Jes's poor behavior.

She was fairly certain her mother was one of those staring, but she hoped Lord Ian was not. When she felt enough time had passed, she chanced a glance at her mother first. She seemed to be engaged in a conversation, thank goodness.

Jes's gaze traveled to Lord Ian. He was speaking to Lady Du'Breven, but when he finished he flicked his attention to Jes. She ducked her head again. The peach ice in her mouth lost its savor and her stomach clenched. If there had ever been a chance of even friendship between them, she had most likely put an end to it with a few pert words. What was wrong with her? Why could she not leave well enough alone with the likes of Bloomsbury and his mother? Must she always try and bring people like them down a notch?

As the desserts were cleared away, the women adjourned to the Crimson Drawing Room to await the men. Jes followed her mother, wishing she could slip away and hide in her bedchambers. It was not as if anyone would miss her. She heaved a heavy sigh. This had the makings of a very long fortnight.

3

GRUDGES OF OLD

"*R*eally, Jes. What did you hope to achieve with that remark?" Her mother had barely closed the door to Jes's chambers before she turned on her. She seemed more confused than angry. "The Bloomsburys are arrogant bores. But they hold a standing within society. You would do well not to offend them." Her mother smirked. "Oh, but we are too late for that little reminder, are we not? You have already done so."

Jes sat down on the window seat with an unladylike thud. "It was not my intent to offend them, Mama. But that woman! Did you see the way she looked down her nose at me? How was I to answer? In the eyes of the ton, we are upstarts from the merchant class. Was I to agree with them and, in the process, shame my own father?"

Lady Rachel sat next to her daughter, placing a gentle hand on her back. "No. Although, it may have been best if you left it alone after saying you did not have an opinion."

Jes opened her mouth to respond, but her mother stopped her with the raise of a hand.

"You do not always need to have the sharper tongue or the last word, dearest. Sometimes it is best to keep quiet."

Leaning her head against the wall, Jes fingered the overlay of her gown. "I know, Mama. But sometimes, I just can't help myself." Her gaze met her mother's. "Especially when I feel they are slighting Papa."

"I understand. But it will not bring him back to us. It will only make your life more difficult."

Jes stood up and moved to the corner. She tugged several times on the bell pull. "I will try harder, Mama. I promise."

She sat down in front of the mirror and removed the rest of the pins from her hair. Looking into the mirror, she caught her mother's eye. There was something that had been on her mind all evening. "Mama? I do not believe you were honest in your remarks about Lady Kendal. Lord Ian did not seem to notice, but I did." She raised her brows.

Lady Rachel returned her daughter's gaze. "I do not know what you are speaking of."

A snort escaped Jes's nose. "Oh Mama, an ice at Gunther's is not as cold as you were when discussing the lady." Jes pursed her lips together. "I know there is a story. Why will you not tell me of it?"

The maid assigned to her by the Countess knocked once on the door and entered, temporarily ending their conversation. Instead, they spoke of things less personal in nature.

The girl dipped a quick curtsy before moving to the wardrobe. She withdrew a nightrail and placed it on the bed. Coming to stand behind Jes, she reached forward and picked up the brush off the table. Without saying a word, she brushed Jes's hair using long strokes. When her hair shone and began to crackle, the maid separated it into three sections and plaited it, draping it over Jes's shoulder.

Jes stood and moved to the side of the bed. The girl worked the buttons loose, then pulled the gown over Jes's head. After easing the stays and removing the chemise, the maid helped Jes into her nightrail.

Looking to Lady Rachel, the girl asked, "May I help you change, my lady?"

Her mother smiled. "Yes, thank you, Fanny. If you would go ready my things, I will be along shortly."

She dipped a curtsy and left the room.

When the door closed, Jes folded her arms across her chest and looked at her mother still seated on the window bench. "You were telling me why you did not like Lady Kendal."

Her mother gave her a slight glare. "Very well. If you must know, Lady Kendal and I were very good friends, before she married Lord Kendal."

Jes's brow furrowed. "Then why were you so cold when you spoke of her?"

Lady Rachel sighed, her eyes taking on a sad gaze. "She married Lord Kendal a few months before I married your father. I attended her wedding...." Her mother looked up at her. "That is how close we were, even though she was closer in age to Lydia. Sadie was in her third season, and probably her last when she met Henry Pinkerton. Although, he was only an earl at the time. I do not believe they loved each other when they married, but it was a good match for both of them. Sadie received a respectable husband and a coveted title. In return, Lord Kendal got a loyal and regal wife."

Lady Rachel fingered the corded edging on the bench cushion. "When the season ended, I returned to Morley and she moved to Penymoor, the residence of the Pinkerton family." She stopped speaking and sat staring at her finger rubbing back and forth over the velvet brocade fabric.

"That is the end of the story? It does not explain your reaction. You have not seen the Countess's daughter in years, yet you still speak of her with warmth and fondness."

Lady Rachel sighed. "As I said, I married your father several months later. Your grandfather was not happy with the match."

Jes nodded her head. "Yes. I am aware of grandfather's feelings on the subject." She had heard this part of the story before. She sat down on the bed and pulled her legs up underneath her.

"The next season—it was just before you were born—your father was traveling. He had one ship then and had not yet made his fortune. Your aunt Lydia invited me to spend the time he was gone with her in London." A wistful sigh sounded from her mother. "I was excited to go, to see my friends again. I had not seen any of them since the previous season."

Jes nodded. "I can imagine. Durham can feel quite isolated."

"Lydia invited me to attend the first ball of the season. It was held at Fallstaff House."

Jes shook her head. "What is Fallstaff House?"

"It was the home of Lord Kendal—Lord Ian's grandfather. I was so excited to see my dear friend, I could hardly sit still in the carriage. We were both married women now. We would have so much to speak of. But when Lydia and Lord Mayfield presented me at the receiving line, Lady Bedford—she had not become a marchioness yet—did not acknowledge our previous acquaintance. She was cold and arrogant. I should have known it would happen. I was naïve." Her mother's voice quieted. "But still it hurt."

Jes closed her gaping mouth. "What was her reason, Mama? Was it because you married Papa?"

Lady Rachel shrugged. "I do not know for sure. She would not speak to me and made it very clear I was not welcome in their home. But it is the only possible cause. We had parted ways the year before on good terms." She sat next to Jes on the bed. Taking her daughter's hand in hers, she patted it softly. "It was my first real experience with the censure my marriage was to bring me. I realized I was no longer a part of the upper crust of English society; I was not even a part of society in general." She heaved a heavy sigh. "My eyes were opened very quickly."

Jes pulled her hand from her mother's. "Oh, Mama. That is terrible. If they could abandon you so completely, they were never truly your friends."

Lady Rachel shook her head. "Oh, Jes. That is what I am trying to make you see. They were my friends. But the ton is the ton and they will not allow anyone to change the rules. I thought I was above the censure because my father was a duke. But my father and mother chose not to stand with me. If my own parents could not do so, why would my friends? They had their own reputations to consider."

Jes looked up into her mother's eyes. "Did any of your friends stay with you?"

Lady Rachel smiled. "Only the Countess's daughter, Alice, was still kind." A small chuckle sounded. "She is very much like her mother. She does not care so much for the opinion of the ton."

Lady Rachel stood abruptly. "You need to rest and I should not keep poor Fanny waiting any longer." She leaned over and gave Jes a quick kiss on the cheek. "I will see you on the morrow, dearest. Sleep tight."

Her mother hurried from the room, leaving Jes to herself and her thoughts.

Was Lord Ian like his mother? Was he so ingrained with the ton, he would not allow an alliance with the likes of her? The daughter of a merchant? A pauper? Jes frowned. From everything she had observed of him in London—he was very much worried about the opinion of society. It was not likely he would ever consider her suitable.

CONRAD CLOSED the door behind him, shrugging out of his coat. He fumbled with the buttons on his waistcoat as he walked towards the large window across the room.

It was dark outside, even though the Countess was keeping country hours. A door opened behind him.

"Let me help you with your cravat, sir."

Conrad turned from the window. "Thank you, Crandall."

The valet worked the knot at Conrad's throat, unwinding the lengthy fabric from around his neck. "Any news from below stairs that I should take note of?"

The servant shook his head. "Not as yet. Give it a few days and I am sure lips will become looser. How was your evening? As dreadful as you anticipated?"

Conrad's brow furrowed as he thought of his answer. "No. Surprisingly, it was quite enjoyable. Have you met an abigail for Lady Rachel or Miss Standish yet?"

Crandall squatted on his haunches, waiting to remove Conrad's boots. Placing a finger to his lips, he looked towards the ceiling. He shook his head. "No one introduced themselves as serving the Standish ladies. I can ask around on the morrow, see what I can determine, if you wish."

Conrad shrugged. He did not know why he even cared. "Just do it discreetly, please."

Crandall gave Conrad a blank stare. "Have I ever been anything but discreet, sir?"

Conrad cringed inwardly. Crandall had been his only valet since before Conrad left for Cambridge. There had never been a reason to doubt Crandall.

"No. You have always been the picture of discretion. I should not have mentioned it." Conrad sighed. "This whole situation—it is making me say and do things which are not in my nature. I don't like it. Ian had better get here soon."

Crandall placed Conrad's boots in the wardrobe and returned with a robe. "Will you be retiring immediately, my lord? Or shall I fetch some tea?" He slipped the robe up Conrad's arms and onto his shoulders, holding the ties out in front of him.

Conrad grabbed the ties and secured them tightly about his waist. He rubbed his eyes, wincing at the scratchy feel of sand beneath his lids. He really should go to bed, but there were a few letters he needed to write. "Send for tea, Crandall. I still have a few hours of work ahead of me."

"Very good, my lord."

Conrad moved to the writing table. Picking up the penknife, he whittled away the sides of the quill until the tip was just as he liked it. He dipped it into the inkwell and poised it over the paper. Flicking the feather up and down on his chin he thought of what he needed to write. Instead of words, the image of Miss Standish entered his mind.

She was intriguing. She was not the most beautiful woman he had seen, but she was lovely. She had much of the same regalness as her mother. But there was something more—something he could not put his finger on. He tried to recall if he had ever heard mention of either of them before. Lady Rachel was undoubtedly the daughter of a duke or a Marquess, which was curious because Conrad knew every duke and marquess in England. And even some in France. But Lady Rachel was unknown to him.

Conrad shifted in his seat. Why he was so concerned with them, he did not know. Crandall was sure to provide him with enough information to satisfy his curiosity. Certainly, that was all his interest in Miss Standish was. Simple curiosity.

He dipped his pen again and scratched out the name of his solicitor on the top of the parchment. All of his earlier aggravation with Ian flooded back. How many times was Conrad going to have to step in to save his reckless brother?

Sometimes Conrad hated being the oldest. The one with all the responsibility. Ian led such a carefree life. Although, if Ian was the eldest, there would be no Pinkerton fortune left. Providence obviously knew how to order them.

The door opened and Crandall brought in a tray with tea and a few biscuits. He set it on a nearby table.

Conrad smiled up at him. "Thank you, Crandall. You may retire for the evening."

"Thank you, my lord. Sleep well." He bowed and left the room, closing the door behind him.

Conrad stood and moved toward the table. Pouring himself a cup of tea, he moved back to his position at the window. The gardens were still lit, the torches casting shadows over the grass and hedges. Miss Standish would look quite lovely in those glowing gardens. Conrad's brow wrinkled. Where did such a thought come from?

He took a long sip of tea and closed his eyes. The burning sensation brought tears into the corners. Slowly he opened them halfway. He set the cup back on the tray.

His letters could wait until morning. For now, he needed to sleep.

4

TALL TALES AND ICY GLARES

*C*onrad left his rooms in the morning feeling restless and discontent. He had received a letter from Ian indicating he would be delayed several days longer. The delay gave Conrad hope that something was to be settled between Ian and Miss Simmons, even if it did prolong his own suffering.

Everyone believed him to be Ian, including the louts Ian called friends, but the whole act was taking a toll on Conrad. He hated the thought that people believed he had the same dissolute character as his brother.

Miss Standish was the only one continually giving him questioning looks. It was as if she knew Ian well, yet Conrad had never heard of the chit until yesterday. A feeling of agitation squeezed his brows together. It was not as if he cared for her opinion, either good or bad. Except, his agitation grew as he realized that was not entirely true. For some unearthly reason, he *did* desire her good opinion.

A loud voice accompanied by a flurry of hushed murmurs reached his ear. Conrad followed the sound, finding a group standing in the Marble Saloon, everyone's necks craned to look at the ceiling. Miss Greystock—dutiful tour guide—described every detail of the intricate plaster. Conrad spotted Miss Standish, slightly apart from the rest of the group, her head cocked back as she listened.

Without understanding why, he smiled and sidled up next to her, dropping his head back as well. "Good morning, Miss Standish. And where is Lady Rachel this morning? Did she not wish to take the tour with you?"

Miss Standish, without dropping her head to glance in his direction, whispered, "She was not feeling well this morning and decided to keep to her room in hopes of recovering enough to attend the musicale tonight."

Everyone turned their heads, looking now at the fireplace. He nodded in understanding. "Being acquainted with the family, she must be familiar with the house." Looking in the same direction as the others, he watched her from the side.

She shook her head, finally looking at him. "Actually, this is the first time she has been to this estate. My mother was acquainted with the family in London."

The group wandered into the next room. Conrad leaned his head toward her. "This room is called the Hounds-coat room. It gets its name because of that portrait hanging over the mantle." He motioned his head in the direction of the painting. "The portrait was painted by van Dyck. It is of the Second Earl's favorite pointer." Conrad was suddenly grateful for Ian's ramblings over the years. "If you wanted a tour, I am convinced I could give you a much more informative one than this." What was he saying? He did not know enough about this house to give her a tour.

Miss Standish tilted her head toward him while her attention was still tuned into Miss Greystock's speech, seemingly trying to pay attention to both conversations. Without shifting her gaze, she whispered. "You know this house well, then?"

"Well enough. Let's just say I know of the more interesting aspects of this house. The ones not on the typical tour."

Miss Winters turned, shushing them with a glare. "Some of us came on this tour with the intent to learn about this grand home. Please do be quiet so we can hear." She turned back toward Miss Greystock, her attention fully engaged on the young lady.

Conrad raised his brows, a laugh twitching at his lips. Miss Standish's lips puckered, whether to laugh or in displeasure, he was not sure. Dipping his head, he tried to school his features into contrition. "Beg pardon, Miss Winters."

Miss Greystock shared some less than fascinating facts about the coffered ceiling and intricate details of the fireplace.

Miss Standish quirked a brow at him. "And what, exactly, are these interesting details Miss Greystock is leaving out?"

Conrad moved in closer, his breath moving the small hairs at the base of her neck. His eyes were drawn to the slope created where neck met shoulder, causing him to stumble on his words. "I, um, I...I could not help but notice Miss Greystock has not mentioned the ghost that haunts these halls."

Miss Standish's brow puckered in confusion, then a single brow raised in...what? Disbelief? Irritation? Conrad had no idea.

"Are you expecting me to believe this home is haunted?"

Conrad shrugged a shoulder. "It is the truth, whether you choose to believe it or not."

A quiet laugh escaped her lips, earning her another glare from Miss Winters. Leaning a little closer into Conrad, which for some ludicrous reason caused his heart rate to increase, she whispered. "And what would this specter look like, Lord Ian? Is he a kind ghost or more the vengeful sort—bent on revenge for past wrongs?"

Looking at the ceiling, Conrad considered the question as he tried to recall all the details Ian had told him over the years. "I have seen it myself." He cringed slightly at the lie. But then, was it a lie if he were speaking as Ian? His brother had claimed to have seen it on several occasions. "It is a young boy who roams the nursery and upper floors on the darkest nights—those with only the slightest hints of a moon."

A quiet chortle puffed from her lips, pushing them out slightly. His breath caught, his gaze transfixed on them.

"I find it difficult to believe such a tale, Lord Ian. Were it true, such a story would be one of the first told."

"The Countess finds the tales vulgar. She would never allow them to be told in a public setting." He placed his hand to the side of his mouth as if sharing a secret with her. "Although, I do believe she secretly finds them piquant."

"Piquant? Interesting choice of words."

"It means..."

She cut him off with a wave of her hand. "I know what it means, my lord. It just is not a word oft spoken." She fixed him with a stare, her brow furrowed.

"Exactly, but it should be. Do you not agree? Perhaps if we use it more over the next few weeks, it will become all the rage."

"Perhaps." Miss Standish's eyes narrowed as she studied him. "The moon is in its waning stage; perhaps a ghost hunt is in order. What say you, Lord Ian? Shall your specter make an appearance and save your reputation or be absent and expose you as a fraud?"

Conrad raised his brows, hoping to hide his sudden discomfort. "Do I detect a challenge, Miss Standish? I believe tomorrow night will be our best opportunity to see it. Will you join me or are you too afraid?" His voice rose on the last word.

Miss Winters turned again, fire burning in her gaze. "Lord Ian, if you please!"

Conrad held up his hands in surrender. Once the ice princess turned her back to him, his shoulders began to shake.

THE GROUP MOVED into the next room. It was yellow, almost to the point of being gaudy. Jes turned curious eyes to Lord Ian. "And what vast knowledge do you have of this room, my lord?" she whispered.

His lips pursed as he glanced around the room. "This is the... um...Yellow Room."

Her lips quirked. "Seems suitable, for a room painted solely in that color. But that is hardly a little-known bit of information."

Lord Ian smirked. "I was just making sure you knew the correct name." He placed his hand under his chin, his finger tapping softly. "This is the room where Edward the First planned his second invasion into Scotland."

Before she could stop it, she snorted out a laugh so loud Miss Greystock stopped speaking and every head turned in their direction. Jes felt the heat all the way to the tips of her ears. "My apologies, Miss Greystock. I seem to have developed a tickle in my throat. Please, carry on." She waved a hand, encompassing the room. "Tell us more about the Yellow Room."

Miss Greystock looked confused. "This is not the yellow room. There is no yellow room in the entirety of this house, that I am aware." Looking around, she nodded her head. "Although I can understand why you would think such a thing." She cast a scowl at Conrad. "Lord Ian must have been talking when I mentioned this was the Painted Drawing Room."

Jes looked at Lord Ian from the corner of her eyes. He appeared to be appropriately repentant until Miss Greystock continued with her tour duties. Then he turned his gaze on her, laughter sparking in his eyes.

A slight smile came unbidden to her lips. But her brow furrowed as she looked at him. He was so different than she had imagined. He was similar to the man she had danced with the one time; the one she had spent hours watching over the rims of glasses or from behind her fan. He had always been light-hearted and charming but in an entirely different way. A way she could not quite define.

He shook his head, tsking quietly. "I am quite certain this has always been named the Yellow Room." He shrugged. "Perhaps they realized how silly it sounded and decided to change it since last I was here."

Her smile increased. "I am sure you are correct, for that does seem to be the most likely scenario." While she was still baffled by him, Jes could not help but like Lord Ian even more. His humor added a depth she had not previously seen. She bit her lower lip in thought. "I was under the impression this house had only been built within the last two hundred years."

Conrad nodded.

"Then you can understand my confusion at Edward I's role in its history."

"Yes, it is a complicated history." He moved to the window and she followed behind. Looking out at the Temple Folly, she spotted Miss Easton and Lord Courtenay and the gaggle of Easton brothers practically running across the lawn. Jes glanced over to Lord Ian, who shrugged. His gaze shifted to the sandstone structure. "It is not widely known, but Ethelred of Wessex planned his attack on the Danes, right there on that plot of ground. The Folly was erected in honor of the great conquest."

She bit her lip as a puff of breath pushed out of her nose, barely stifling a laugh. "I am beginning to think it is not just this house you know nothing about, but our entire history. The battle against the Danes happened in Berkshire, my lord."

Looking at her as if she were daft, he guffawed. "Everyone knows that, Miss Standish. As I said, the little-known fact is that the planning was done here in Yorkshire. Please, keep up." His tone was condescending, mocking even.

She narrowed her eyes at him and thought a look of uncertainty might have crossed his face. His smile faltered. A protective feeling reared up inside her. She knew that same feeling. "I believe you are mistaken, for everyone knows that particular folly was constructed because it is the exact place Hercules defeated the Cyclopes army threatening to overrun the Britons."

Lord Ian's mouth curved into a grin. Nodding he added, "Ah, I do believe you are correct. It is the site of the Rockingham Obelisk where Ethelred made his plans. Thank you, Miss Standish, for correcting me." Her heart stuttered at the look of complete joy on his face. She had always thought Lord Ian handsome, but at this moment she could not think of a single man—gentle or noble—able to rival him.

They both broke out laughing, stopping suddenly when they realized they were alone. She looked about the empty room. How had they not noticed everyone leaving? Walking quickly to the doorway, they peered into the hallway, straining to hear Miss Greystock's voice. Her voice carried down the corridor, allowing them to follow it until they found the correct room.

Lord Ian peered inside. "If we walk in now, everyone in attendance will take notice. It will, no doubt, cause quite a scene. While I care nothing about the opinions of others, you may not have such a luxury."

She bit her lower lip again, wishing she held such a position. "Is there no other way in?"

He peered into the room again. "Perhaps if we listen, we can wait for a time when their backs will be turned and sneak in then."

She shrugged her shoulder. "There is another option."

His brows rose. "Yes? Do go on, Miss Standish."

"We could abandon the house in favor of the gardens. From what I have been told, they are rich in ancient history." Her lips twitched and her brows rose.

He shrugged. "There are many parts of the grounds I have yet to tell you about." Just then, he heard Miss Greystock mention the next room. Grabbing her hand, Lord Ian tugged her into the alcove of a nearby doorway. Jes nearly tripped as butterflies took flight in her stomach and then flew into her legs, making them wobbly and weak.

He moved in front of her but kept her hand in his. Peeking around the corner, he watched until the last person exited the room. Pulling her behind him, they quietly took up the rear of the group. He leaned in and whispered in her ear. "Perhaps we can save the grounds for another day. There is still much I have not told you about the house."

Jes shivered at his closeness, barely able to contain the excitement she felt. What stories would he make up next?

5

RESCUING A DAMSEL, NOT IN DISTRESS

*J*es had been disappointed to find Lord Ian seated at the far end of the dining table. She had thoroughly enjoyed the house tour and had hoped to continue the conversation at dinner. Fortune, it seemed, was not smiling upon her, as she was seated again by Lord Bloomsbury. Not only did he continually flip his sweat-soaked hair around, but he seemed to have a problem with spittle. It flew from his mouth with any use of a word containing s. His sense of over importance had rendered her quite speechless throughout the meal. Considering her outburst the last time they were seated near each other, it seemed for the best.

Now, standing in the back of the Grand Drawing room or the Green Pianoforte room, as Lord Ian claimed, she looked at the other guests. She spotted Lord Bloomsbury just as he noticed her. Determined to put at least a room's length between them, she ducked her head and spun around into a solid chest. Raising her face, her eyes locked with Lord Ian's, a smile coming naturally to her face.

"You look to be fleeing from something. Pray, what has caused such discomfort?" He scanned the room.

Dropping her chin to her chest, she sighed. "Lord Bloomsbury caught my eye. I fear he is on his way to find me. I had hoped my comments at dinner the other night might have deterred his attentions."

Lord Ian chuckled. "Ah, yes. Bloomsbury would cause even the most fearless to retreat." He held out his arm, moving towards the refreshment table as she grasped the lifeline. Casting a look over his shoulder, he tsked. "It would seem he is determined to speak with you."

"I do not know why. I know his mother does not approve of me." Jes clutched his arm. "Please, do not leave me to him. I have already suffered through his conversation tonight."

"I wouldn't dream of abandoning you." He handed her a cup of lemonade.

Just then the baron came to a stop in front of them. She grimaced as his hair continued its forward progression, dangling down into his face. Flipping it back into place, droplets of sweat flew in all directions. He dabbed at his forehead.

"If you will excuse us, Lord Ian. I was on my way over to speak with Miss Standish when you interrupted." Lord Bloomsbury looked up his pointed nose at Lord Ian.

"I cannot, Bloomsbury, for she sat beside you at dinner. You had plenty of time to converse. Perhaps you would do better to find someone else to bless with your insights this evening." He turned to her, placing his hand on the small of her back. Warmth spread out from where his hand rested, up into her arms and chest. He gently pushed her away from the refreshment table. "Come, Miss Standish. I believe your mother has arrived. I shall deliver you to her side." They left the baron babbling behind them.

Jes's heart hammered. This was the Lord Ian of her imaginings

—coming to her rescue when she needed it. Their exchange this morning had given her even more to admire.

She sat down next to her mother. "Mama, how are you feeling?"

Lady Rachel patted her on the cheek. "I am feeling much recovered, Jes." Her voice came out scratchy and weak.

Jes narrowed her eyes. Lady Rachel ignored the penetrating stare, lifting her gaze to Lord Ian. "Ah, Lord Ian. If you are not otherwise engaged, we would be honored if you would join us for the musical selections."

A smile stretched across his face. "I can think of nothing I would like better. Thank you, my lady." He sat down next to Jes, stretching out his long, lean legs. A small sigh sounded before Jes could stop it. She flicked her gaze back to her own lap, where her hands furiously twisted the ends of her shawl, her mouth pinched shut.

She felt him move beside her, his breath touching her neck as he leaned in. "Tell me, Miss Standish. Your Christian name is quite unusual. Pray, what are its origins? It sounds vaguely familiar somehow."

Her brow puckered. Why was he asking her this again? "Do you not remember?"

***

CONRAD SAT UP STRAIGHT, running his hands down his thighs. "Remember?" Gah! This must have been something she had already spoken to Ian about.

"Yes, you asked me the same question in London."

He took a long breath, his eyes looking everywhere but at her. How was he supposed to smooth this over? He let out an awkward laugh. "I was kicked in the head by my horse, some time ago. I am

42

afraid I lost a bit of memory." His made-up stories had worked on the house tour; perhaps it would now, as well. A small smile turned his lips as he thought about the absurd stories they made up while touring the house.

Her brow furrowed, an action he was finding increasingly adorable. But there was a look in her eyes he was unsure about. Was it hurt? Uncertainty? Whatever it was, it was not good.

She leaned to the side. "I am so sorry. I had no idea." One brow rose in challenge. "Tell me, my lord, was that before or after Shakespeare wrote Macbeth in the White Daisy room?"

He smiled guiltily. "After, most assuredly. Would you mind telling me the story again? It was a very long time ago when I first heard it."

When she smiled, his breath came out in a soft whoosh.

"It was my mother's idea. She is a great admirer of Shakespeare. The name Jessica is from The Merchant of Venice." Miss Standish gave a little tilt of her head as her shoulder shrugged. How could such a movement cause his stomach to turn to porridge?

"That would explain why it sounded familiar. I too, share your mother's appreciation."

The Countess stood, causing all conversations to drop to a whisper and then, to silence. It seemed the musicale was to begin. Conrad used all his control to pull his gaze away from Miss Standish. The Countess asked Miss Barton to start the evening's performances. Conrad was mildly impressed with the young lady's talent. More than polite applause sounded as she completed her piece.

"Next, we would be honored to hear from Miss Standish, if you please." The Countess looked expectantly at her.

Jes stood up, smiling. "Of course, I shall be happy to sing a number."

A small rumble of whispers started. Her mother placed a hand on Jes's arm. "You do not have to do this, dearest. I cannot sing with you and I know how much you dislike singing by yourself."

Patting her mother's hand, she began to make her way out of their row of seats. "I will be fine, Mama."

As she started up the aisle, Conrad heard her mother murmuring. "All is not well. Is there no way to stop her?" Lady Rachel looked as if she was going to be ill. Miss Standish whispered her song choice to Miss Marleigh, who began to play the introduction. Taking her own sheet music, Jes began to sing. The sound pouring out dropped his mouth open.

Sitting forward in his seat, Conrad now understood Lady Rachel's apprehension. He had heard stray cats with a better sense of tone than Miss Standish.

Miss Marleigh seemed to have a difficult time playing, the howling most assuredly causing a break in her concentration. Whispers spread throughout the crowd. Conrad even heard a few quiet giggles.

A surge of defensiveness gripped him. But what could he do? Without thinking, he stood and moved down the aisle, joining in on the second verse. He tried to sing a little louder, hoping to deflect some of the attention onto himself, but she increased her volume. From the corner of his eye, he could see Lord Anthony and Mr. Beauchamp barely stifling laughs. Even the Easton men seemed to be struggling to keep their composure. Conrad was finding it difficult to keep his own voice in tune. Then Miss Standish dropped her voice an octave, although it was still badly off key. His only option was to drop his and try to match it as best he could. By the last stanza, Miss Standish began to falter, missing notes and a few words, but finally, the song came to an end. The room was silent, as people looked back and forth between one another. Then the Countess began to clap. Slowly, one by one, other awkward claps began to sound.

Lady Du'Brevan stood and cleared her throat. "Well, that was...something, was it not?" She looked around the room expectantly. When no one answered, she continued on. "Let us now hear from Miss Winters."

Conrad tried to escort Miss Standish back to her seat, but she rushed ahead of him. She sat down next to her mother, her breath coming out in short bursts. As soon as he retook his seat, she turned on him, whispering in apparent outrage, "What were you doing? Can you not stand to have someone else receive attention, my lord?" He looked at her as confusion settled in. She was angry with him? After he had tried to save her from utter humiliation? He had expected at least a quiet thank you, but not the daggers hurling from her current gaze.

Several people on the row in front of them turned in their seats, giving her cross stares. Her mother looked at the two of them, eyes large and lips pursed. Miss Standish faced forward in her seat. He could feel her body shaking next to him.

Lady Rachel's gaze never left her daughter. At last, he heard applause. Lady Rachel began to cough, quietly at first but then building in volume. She looked over to Miss Standish and motioned for her to get up. Complying, she stood and turned to help her mother from the room. Once they had left, Conrad waited for the next performer to finish her piece. He heard none of it and could not even say the name of the young lady, his thoughts were so entirely on Miss Standish.

As the last strains sounded from the pianoforte, Conrad stood and moved to the refreshment table. He grabbed two cups and slipped into the empty hallway. Walking quietly, he struggled to determine which room they had entered. Finally, he heard a muffled sound in the room across the hall. Pushing the door open with his toe, he peered into a drawing room. Miss Graystock had undoubtedly told him its name, but he had been so preoccupied, he could only remember his made up name—the Indian Rug room. Miss Standish sat on the settee, her mother next to her, rubbing circles on her back. Miss Standish's face lay cradled in her hands. She did not appear to be wracked with sobs, which seemed a good thing.

Conrad moved forward a few steps, drawing the attention of Lady Rachel.

"Ah, Lord Ian." She motioned him inside.

All of a sudden, he felt very conspicuous and out of place. This was a moment for mother and daughter. He should not have intruded. "I just came to bring you a drink for your cough." His eyes darted to Miss Standish. She had raised her head. Her eyes were red and slightly puffy. So she had been crying. The knowledge rooted Conrad in place. He wanted to rush over and comfort her, but he also wanted to flee, to avoid the emotions surging through him. He wanted this tightness in his chest to go away.

"Thank you, my lord. I seem to be recovered for the moment." Lady Rachel gave her daughter a small nudge.

Miss Standish looked over to him. "I have been informed I owe you an apology." She swallowed hard and glanced at her mother. "It would seem I am not an accomplished singer, nor have I ever been." There was a slight edge to her voice on the last words. Her mother colored slightly. "I am sorry for my outburst and accusations. I was not aware, at the time, you were trying to help me."

Their gazes locked and Conrad felt himself moving towards her. Reaching the settee, he glanced quickly at Lady Rachel, thrusting a cup at her, a few drops landing on his hand. "My lady, your lemonade." His gaze returned to Miss Standish. "I brought one for you as well. I thought perhaps..."

She smiled, actually smiled after all that had happened. It

made him want to reach out to her all the more. "You thought perhaps my poor performance was due to a dry throat?"

He shrugged, a small smile tugging the corners of his mouth. Unable to pull his gaze from her, he whispered, "It was not so terrible."

Miss Standish laughed again. "That is precisely what started this whole farce. If people had been honest with me from the beginning," she looked pointedly at her mother, "this entire scene could have been avoided." Her hands twisted at the fringe on her shawl. "Although, we would never have heard your rich baritone voice." She watched him through her lashes. "And that may well be worth it all, don't you agree, Mama?"

Conrad did not understand what he was feeling. He cleared his throat and bowed. "I am glad to have been of service to you, Miss Standish. I shall leave you to your mother's care and bid you both good evening." He turned and strode into the hallway. His heart raced and he knew he could not return to the musicale, but his chambers held nothing for him either. Perhaps an evening ride could clear his mind and sort out his jumbled emotions.

6

GOSSIP AND GHOSTS

Conrad leaned against the wall, swirling the amber liquid in his glass. So many thoughts battled for attention, his brain felt a bit like the brandy in his hand. He had received word his sister had taken ill. The letter has said his presence was not necessary, yet it still weighed on his mind.

Looking around the smoke-filled room, he continued the circular motion with his hand. They would be joining the ladies in the parlor soon and, if truth be told, the letter was not the only thing occupying his thoughts. His chest tightened as her face came to his mind.

Miss Standish had been noticeably absent from the day's activities, whether the result of the performance the night before or her mother's health, he could not be sure. But whatever the reason, he missed her. He wasn't sure when her presence had become so important, but it was there. True and undeniable.

Conrad heard someone call Ian's name. He sighed, tired of the charade. Turning toward the sound, he groaned inwardly. Mr. Beauchamp and Lord Anthony stood off to the side with a new member of the house party. A full-on growl rumbled in Conrad's throat. Mr. Teirny. The men sauntered over, stopping when they reached Conrad's side.

"Teirny," Conrad said. He tried to look cordial, even happy to see the man, but his mouth refused to turn upward. "When did you arrive?"

Teirny looked at him, disapproval on his face. "Last evening, just before the musicale. Or perhaps the strangled cat performance is a more accurate name. It was fortunate others with talent were able to salvage the evening."

Beauchamp raised his eyebrows but said nothing. Lord Anthony chuckled softly, lifting his glass to his mouth. Before putting it to his lips he muttered, "It is fortunate she has such a pretty face or she would never survive the ton."

Conrad knit his brows together. How would Ian respond? Would he join in the mocking or defend Miss Standish? Conrad hoped Ian would never stoop to the likes of Teirny, but he truly had no idea. Which made him sad for an entirely different reason. "She performed once in London a few seasons ago. Were any of you present?"

Lord Anthony laughed again and Teirny smirked. It was Beauchamp who spoke up this time. "We were all there. Do you not remember? Her London performance was only just better than last night." Beauchamp winced at his words. "But apart from her singing, she is a lovely creature." At that moment Beauchamp rose a few notches in Conrad's esteem.

Lord Anthony's brows rose. "And, from what I've heard, she is swimming in lard."

Teirny snorted. "Your information is old news. My understanding is they haven't a sixpence to scratch with." He glanced over to Conrad as if he had three heads. "How can *you* not remember that performance? You were her harshest critic. I believe you compared her to a gaggle of squawking geese!" Teirny laughed loudly, sloshing his port onto the rug and drawing the attention of those around them.

Conrad shrank back, trying to blend into the wallpaper, heat rising up his neck. He had known his brother was a rake, but his churlish nature was disappointing news. "I barely remember the chit. Perhaps Conrad is beginning to rub off on me." He forced a chuckle. "Who knows, I may even forsake women *and* wagers." Pretending to laugh uproariously with them, he tried to come up with an excuse to leave. Looking around, his gaze landed on Lord Courtenay. "I need to refill my glass. If you'll excuse me, gentleman."

Before he could escape, Lord Anthony grabbed his arm. "You have barely touched your brandy." Eying him, Lord Anthony asked. "What were you about all day, Pinkerton? I thought you were to come to the picnic this afternoon."

"It was my plan also, but at the last minute I was called upon by the Countess." In truth, when he had seen Miss Standish was not among those gathering for the outing, he had decided the event was not worth his time. "She was in need and I volunteered my services."

The three men laughed again uproariously, obviously already in their cups. Conrad frowned until their interpretation of his words hit him. The growl actually escaped this time. "I went into town to fetch some powders from the apothecary." He shook his head. What a bunch of commonplace minds. He nodded across the room. "Conrad asked me to relay a message to Lord Courtenay for him. I had forgotten until this very moment. Gentlemen." Turning away from the louts, he mumbled to himself. "I do not understand why Ian calls you friends."

"What was that, Ian?" Teirny asked Conrad's back. "Be careful, people might begin to confuse you with your brother." Again, they laughed loudly.

Conrad tossed a smirk over his shoulder and continued in the direction of Lord Courtenay. He did not really have much to say to the man, especially while pretending to be his bacon-brained brother. But anything was better than continuing to participate in the other conversation. As he approached, Conrad tried to look properly uninterested. "Lord Courtenay. I did not expect to find you at this gathering."

Courtenay leveled his gaze, scrutinizing him. Conrad had been working closely with him on reform measures for the upcoming session of Parliament. It was a volatile subject and one they tried to keep between those they knew were on their side, at least until the details were worked out.

Ian would never bother himself with something so wholly unconcerned with himself as reform, so Conrad had to make it appear the conversation was of no interest to him. "Conrad made me memorize it exactly." He heaved a heavy sigh of irritation. "He is notoriously picksome."

From the look of impatience on Courtenay's face, he believed he was speaking to Ian. Courtenay waved his hand in the air. "Yes, yes. What is it?"

Conrad raised his voice. "'Shearsby...'"

Courtenay cut him off with a glare and snapped. "Lower your voice, man."

With wide eyes, Conrad leaned in close. "I beg your pardon, my lord. Conrad said 'Shearsby is with us. We can meet with him in the coming months to discuss things further.'" Conrad took a step back. "That is it? That is all of the message?" He narrowed his eyes at Courtenay. "What does it mean, anyway? Conrad would not tell me."

"It is not something to be discussed...here." He nodded in the direction of Lord Anthony, Mr. Beauchamp, and Mr. Teirny.

"Is there a message I should pass on to my brother?"

Shaking his head, Courtenay drained the last of his glass. "No. I shall send a messenger with any information for Lord Kendal." He turned to leave, but then turned back. "Thank you for delivering the message. I was afraid something had happened when I had not heard anything from Kendal."

Conrad's frustration grew. Not only was he stuck acting like Ian, now he would not know what Courtenay had discovered for several days more. Conrad set his untouched glass on the side table, following the others to the parlor to join the women. Relief filled him when he saw Miss Standish sitting with a group of young ladies. Her head was tilted back in an inappropriate and utterly charming laugh. His stomach danced at the thought of spending the late night hours seeking out an elusive ghost with her.

LIGHTNING LIT up the hallway through the large window. The rain, pelting against the glass, added to the chilling mood. Jes gave a small shiver as she thought about where they were going. It was quite possibly the most preposterous thing she had ever done. Pray, who in their right mind went traipsing about a very large, very old home in the middle of the night? Searching for ghosts, no less. A chuckle burst out, turning Miss Barton's frightened eyes on her.

"Maybe we should return to our chambers, Miss Standish. I am beginning to think this is not such a clever idea." There was a slight quiver to the poor girl's voice.

Jes stifled a sigh of annoyance. The girl was a milkweed, a trait

Jes found difficult to tolerate in large quantities. But she liked Miss Barton well enough. After all, she did tend to attract Lord Blooms-bury's attention enough to keep him away from Jes. Tucking her hand around Miss Barton's arm, she essentially dragged her along the hallway. "Come now, Miss Barton. You are sure to be married before the end of the next season. Take your chance at some fun before the leg shackle is locked for good."

Word had spread that the group would meet in the Statuary Hall. Entering the room, Jes could hear the murmuring of voices. The two girls looked around the crowd. While Miss Barton had not confided it in her, Jes was quite certain the girl had a tendre for Mr. Julius Easton. As suspected, Miss Barton's gaze immediately sought him out. She slowly and gently began to tug Jes in his direc-tion. Turning her head this way and that, Jes tried to find Lord Ian. Whose idea had it been to meet amid all these statues? As they passed several sculptures in various degrees of undress, she finally caught sight of him. He was speaking to Lord Davies. Her pulse quickened and her stomach danced excitedly. She dropped her hand from around Miss Barton's arm, moving in a different direction.

Worried Lord Ian would sense her anxiousness to see him, she feigned interest in the marble next to him, looking altogether too interested in the detailed carving of the feet on the Juno sculpture by Joseph Nollekens.

Behind her, a grunt sounded. She pretended to pull herself away from the piece, looking up into Lord Ian's pale green eyes.

"I was beginning to wonder if you were too pigeon-livered to come."

Jes felt her lips begin to quiver. "Pigeon-livered, my lord? I believe I have only heard that term one other time, and I am quite certain the speaker was not a gentleman." She arched a brow, hoping he would see it as a challenge.

Lord Ian smiled, matching her cocked brow. "Are you accusing me of ungentlemanly behavior, Miss Standish?"

She shook her head. "Never, my lord. Just introducing a story. I know how much you love a good one."

With a half-smile and a sparkle in his eye, he leaned in. "I am most anxious to hear your tale. Let us get this adventure started and you can regale me once we are underway."

He turned to the group, drawing everyone's attention to him. "I believe we are all here. Let us make our way to the nursery wing. Everyone take a candle. The halls where we are going will not be lit. And please, keep your voices to a whisper for the sake of the other guests, as well as any ghosts."

A few snickers could be heard from behind, but from whom Jes did not know. Her eyes stayed firmly fixed on Lord Ian. Her stomach felt as if a million butterflies waited to break free. Her gaze broke only when Wellington, the Countess's pug, trotted over and began to paw at her slippers. Looking down at him, she picked the little dog up and scratched him behind the ears.

The group began to move in a swarm towards the stairway. Jes lowered the dog to the floor, noticing Miss Barton had returned to her side. Two of the Easton men followed several paces behind. Mr. Julius Easton looked mildly disinterested, while Mr. Tauney Easton was engaged in a conversation with Miss Anne Townshend, his hands waving wildly as he spoke. Miss Anne watched his every movement, nearly tripping when they began to climb the stairs. Jes stifled her laughter until she stumbled on the stair as well.

Strong hands gripped her upper arms, stopping her from falling. When she looked up and found Lord Ian's face, she almost tripped again. He made sure she was steady on her feet before releasing her. "I believe you were about to spin me a yarn of questionable origin."

She smiled, something that seemed to happen without much coaxing whenever he was near. His request, she waved aside. "I find I am more interested in stories of a more ethereal nature."

"Very well." He shrugged. "I assume this is your first encounter with an..." His voice dropped to a whisper as he wiggled his fingers in the air. "Apparition?"

Jes let out a dramatic sigh. "Indeed. But this is not your first time with this particular ghost, I remember. Tell me, my lord, have you seen spirits other places as well?"

"I see them everywhere. It is as if they follow me." An exaggerated grimace passed briefly over his face.

She tried to give him a bland expression, but the anticipation was too much and her grin broke forth. "What is the story behind this ghost? Surely you know all the intricacies."

Miss Barton scooted in closer. "Truly, there is a story?"

Jes glanced over, trying not to scowl at the girl for intruding on the moment she felt she was having with Lord Ian. Her stomach burned when he turned his attention to her friend.

"Indeed. There is always a story where ghosts are concerned." His gaze returned to Jes and her envy melted away, pooling on the floor with every word he spoke. Surely, he did not look at every young lady in this way, did he? "The story goes like this. One of the old earls was hosting a house party, similar to this very one. At breakfast on the first morning, one of the young ladies lamented she had scarce slept a wink. She contended something cold had awakened her with a kiss."

Miss Barton squeaked, sucking in her breath, eyes wide as saucers. They came to a stop on the stairs. Jes glared at her. "Really, Miss Barton. A little tenacity."

Jes returned her gaze to Lord Ian, noticing the slight tremor in his lips. "Please continue, my lord." She began to move back up the staircase.

He nodded. "The former earl dismissed the young woman's claims, attributing them to the dramatics of a young woman. After numerous sleepless nights, the girl insisted on different sleeping chambers. Grudgingly, the earl agreed and the young lady did not complain about her sleep again. Once the party had ended and the guests all removed themselves to their own estates, the earl had the walls of the room in question searched. When nothing came of it, he ordered the floor removed, revealing..." Lord Ian paused, merriment dancing in his eyes. "A small casket."

This time it was Jes who sucked in her breath. She was totally unaware of anyone but the two of them at that moment. "No! I can scarce believe it." She gripped the handrail, once again halting their upward progression. "Whose was it?"

"It is true." He looked as though he was on the verge of laughter. "It was discovered the wooden box belonged to a boy of eight or nine, the youngest son of a previous earl, who drowned after falling into an icy pond."

"Why was it placed under the floorboards of the guest room?" Jes barely recognized her own voice. Her heart pounded in her chest.

His voice dropped to match her own whispered tone. "That, my dear Miss Standish, is the mystery. No one seems to know exactly when or how the casket came to be under the bedroom." Their gazes locked and her palms began to sweat inside her gloves.

Lord Ian motioned her up the remaining stairs, the rest of the group coming up behind them. "Once the coffin was removed, the boy's spirit seemed to stay behind. From that time on, he could be found roaming the halls outside the nursery."

The group finally arrived at top of the staircase. Lord Ian squinted down the hallway as another slice of lightning brightened the corridor. The thunder quickly followed. "If I remember correctly..." He looked in the other direction, but then turned back, looking for anything Ian had told him which might indicate the direction they should go. "This is the way to the nursery." He looked at everyone, his face very serious. "I suggest keeping close together." He held his arm out for Jes to take hold.

She wrapped her hand around his muscled upper arm, momentarily pulled from the lingering jitters caused by the story. "Is this necessary, my lord? Do you believe we could be in danger?" She tried to keep the shiver from her voice, afraid he would realize fear was not what put it there.

A sly grin turned his lips, his brows wiggling a few times. "We cannot be too careful, Miss Standish. And what would I tell your mother if something should happen to you?" He covered her hand with his own, drawing her gaze down. Her breath caught in her throat.

A yelp sounded and Wellington scurried past her in the opposite direction.

Her candle flickered, then extinguished completely. Jes glanced behind them, noticing several other candles had blown out as well. The few that burned caused eerie shadows to dance on the wall. She moved her candle, hoping to light it off Lord Ian's just as his puffed out and the hallway went dark.

She heard a shuffle next to her, then felt a warm breath on her earlobe.

"Do you see him?" Lord Ian's voice was a whisper, but it still caused the hair on her neck to stand on end and gooseflesh to appear. Or maybe it was the hazy white figure of a young boy clinging to the nursery doorframe.

7

CHURCH HISTORY

*J*es looked about the Pillared Hall, feigning interest in the architecture. If asked, she could not recite the color of a single pillar, let alone any commentary on their structure or form. Her mind was, instead, full of ghosts and the strong arms of a certain lord. She shook her head for at least the twentieth time that morning. While she had been imagining for years a relationship with Lord Ian, in her mind she had known it was very unlikely. But now, it was not only happening, but it was also better than even she had believed it could be.

At least from her point of view. And that is what bothered her. She knew her feelings, had known them since London. But she did not know his. The way he paid her such special attention, she believed he felt something for her, but the degree of his attachment was the question that plagued her.

Jes tried to tell herself they still had more than a week for things to work themselves out, but something nagged at her. Something in her mind told her things were not what they seemed.

"Did I mention da Vinci carved each and every one of these

pillars? It was before he carved David and his other more famous pieces."

Jes looked over her shoulder, unable to hide the smile on her face. "Really. He started by carving pillars?"

Lord Ian nodded, a look of incredulity on his face. "Of course. One does not carve David on their first attempt. These were his practice carvings."

"Practice carvings. I see." She nodded. "I do not believe the Countess would appreciate you calling her pillars practice pieces." She pulled her eyes from him and looked at the dozens of pillars holding up the floor above. "This room is truly amazing. Did you not say this was also where Cleopatra first met Marc Anthony?" She laughed at his serious expression. "I do not believe many Englishman understand what a historical treasure they have here."

Lord Ian nodded. "It is true. You are lucky to be one of the few to know of its greatness."

A footman entered the hall and announced the carriages were ready. Jes looked about and spotted her mother coming toward them. Jes marveled at her mother. She always walked with such grace and dignity. No one would ever know she was in a hurry to meet them. It was no wonder her father had fallen in love with this lady. Jes wished she had a fraction of the decorum her mother did.

Lord Ian bowed to Lady Rachel. "My lady, may I escort you and your lovely daughter to church?"

Her mother nodded. "Thank you, my lord." The slight tightness in her mother's expression did not escape Jes's notice. It was not the first time she had seen the reaction when her mother spoke to him. Jes did not know if it was suspicion due to his mother or displeasure by what she saw in him. The severity had softened since Lord Ian's attempt to help her at the musicale but had not disappeared completely.

Lord Ian held out an arm to each lady and walked them to the waiting carriages. A line of people stood waiting, as each carriage filled and another pulled forward. Their little group brought up the end of the line. Jes smiled at the thought of it just being the three of them on the ride to the chapel.

The line quickly faded and soon Lord Ian was handing both Jes and her mother up into the carriage. He climbed in behind them and sat across from her. The door was closing when a shout came from outside.

"Hold the carriage."

Jes cringed. She knew to whom the voice belonged. As suspected, Lady Bloomsbury entered the carriage, followed closely by her son. Jes's lips fluttered as she expelled a deep breath. This was not to be the pleasant ride she had hoped for. The carriage was quiet, each person looking out their respective window, except Lady Bloomsbury. She looked straight ahead, a scowl on her face.

The carriage rolled to a stop on the drive of an old church, waiting for their turn to disembark. Gravestones dotted the yard outside her window. Many looked very old, with moss and lichens covering much of the writing on the stones. A low stone wall encircled the grounds. "Oh, it is so lovely." Jes put her fingers to the window.

"Some of those tombstones date back to the 1400s." Lord Ian looked from the churchyard to her.

The carriage rolled forward several rods and the church came into view. The stones of the building were an orange-red color. Streaks of black and gray ran down the stone fronts, deposits from centuries of rain and elements, toning down the color.

"This church was originally a chapel-of-ease to Wath. It dates back to the early 1200s. One of the earls in the late 1400's altered it by adding pillars for a new aisle. You can see it there." He pointed out the window to a section of the church.

Jes looked at him, her brows furrowed. "I cannot tell if you are making this up or if it is actually part of the history."

He shrugged, a brow raised, further adding to her confusion. "By the late 1600s the family added on again. More space was needed to fit the memorials the earl had commissioned to honor his ancestors. The largest monument is to the first earl, who was beheaded on Tower Hill by Charles I."

Jes was mesmerized. Lord Ian was more than just a handsome gentleman who could weave an extraordinary tale. "These stories are far too ordinary. They must be real." Jes leaned forward, placing her elbows on her knees and her chin in her hands.

Her mother cleared her throat and Jes looked over to see her discreetly shaking her head.

Jes sat back up, smoothing her dress in front of her. "What else do you know of this little chapel?"

Lord Ian put a finger to his lips. "Let's see..." The carriage lurched forward as it moved closer to the chapel entrance. "The tower holds six bells and the clock is the first I have seen with only one hand."

Jes leaned over to the window and peered out at the clock tower. She let out a small gasp when she saw he was correct.

"I almost forgot to mention the most important information." His brow quirked again and Jes felt her lips begin to twitch. She knew what was coming next.

"Do you see that large headstone, there in the middle?" He had leaned closer to her, their knees almost touching. "That is the very spot where Emperor Constantine declared Catholicism the state religion."

Jes laughed as Lord Bloomsbury huffed from the opposite corner. She had nearly forgotten he and his mother were in the carriage with them.

"That is absurd, my lord." Bloomsbury then turned his gaze to

Jes. "I cannot believe a girl of your sense should believe such a falsehood."

Lord Ian winked at Jes, earning him a gasp from Lady Bloomsbury.

"My dear Lord Bloomsbury. I beg your pardon. The tale is merely a joke between the Standish ladies and myself."

Lady Bloomsbury leveled a glare at Lord Ian. "Then you should keep your remarks to the three of you and not involve respectable people in your lies."

Jes pressed her lips together tightly, feeling all the blood drain from them, in an effort to stop the laughter rumbling around in her chest.

Lord Ian looked the picture of contrition. "Correct, as always, my lady." He bowed as well as he could while sitting in a carriage. "My apologies."

Lady Bloomsbury sniffed and turned her head away from him.

The carriage moved forward again, but this time the door opened and the step was placed. Lord Ian climbed out quickly then waited to hand her out. Jes sat, allowing her mother to go first, but Lady Bloomsbury shot Lady Rachel a glare. "You are not the ranking member of this carriage Lady Rachel."

Jes felt her head snap back as if she had been slapped. She looked over to her mother, who sat serenely on the bench, a soft smile on her lips. "After you, my lady."

Lord Bloomsbury followed close behind his mother, glancing over his shoulder at Jes before he exited the carriage.

"How do you maintain such a countenance with someone like her?" Jes whispered loudly.

Her mother smiled and patted Jes's hand. "Oh, dearest. You cannot let the likes of the Bloomsburys ruin your peace. There are more people like them than not." She straightened her hair and dress. "I have had years of practice. It bothered me at first, but I made my choice and I regret very little. Now, Lord Ian has been waiting for quite some time. I think it best if we relieve him of his duty and remove ourselves from this carriage."

Jes eying her mother for any indication she was masking her true feelings. When she saw none, she nodded her head. Lady Rachel stood and grasped Lord Ian's hand as she stepped down. Jes followed behind, feeling the heat of his hand as he grasped hers. Once both her feet were firmly planted on the ground, she expected him to release her hand. When he didn't, she looked up into his face.

He took a deep breath. Placing her hand on his arm he began to walk towards her mother.

Her stomach jumped and her heart stuttered. What did this mean?

Lord Ian led them up the few steps and into the church. The interior of the chapel was much darker compared with the bright sunshine outside. Jes squinted as she looked around her. Several marble monuments lined the walls, carvings of people kneeling over altars. Some depicted the men only, but most showed the lords and their ladies. A large stained glass window stood at the front of the room, dust motes fluttering about every time the door opened and closed.

The benches were mostly filled. Only a few pews at the back were open. Lord Ian led them over to one on the right, allowing Lady Rachel to enter first, followed by Jes. He sat next to her at the end.

The vicar began his sermon and Jes settled in to listen. At least she intended to listen, but every time Lord Ian shifted beside her, her attention drifted to him. When he leaned into her, she felt her body move closer to him. His voice was barely a whisper. He nodded his head in the direction of the vicar. "Did you know that is the very spot where John Wesley preached in 1733?"

Jes looked from the vicar to Lord Ian. Today was another glimpse into this man she was growing fonder of every day. She had had a childish affection for him since the first time she had seen him, but her feelings were changing, growing into something more...mature? She was not yet able to define what she felt, but she could not deny it was there.

He motioned with his head to the side aisle. "And there is where King Henry wrote his Declaration of the Seven Sacraments Against Martin Luther."

Jes put her hand to her mouth, a snort sounding from behind her fingers. Several people on the bench in front of them turned in her direction. Her mother placed a hand on her leg, squeezing it lightly.

"I do not believe God would approve of you making light of his holy chapel," Jes whispered back.

Lord Ian kept his head cocked to the side, while his eyes stayed forward, locked on the vicar. "I disagree. I believe God sees the humor in many things. How could he bestow it upon others if he himself does not have it?"

Jes's brow creased. She had never thought of God in such a way. Her vicar in Durham would surely consider such sentiments heresy, but Jes felt they had at least a hint of truth to them.

She leaned into him, her bonnet brushing against his temple. Turning to face him, their gazes locked. She swallowed, the voice of the vicar fading into the background.

"Perhaps it is a conversation for a different place," Lord Ian whispered. "We would not want to disrupt those worshiping around us." His eyes never left hers.

Jes nodded.

Her mother squeezed her leg again and Jes was brought back to the church and the vicar's sermon.

She faced forward, her breathing feeling shallow and fast. She dropped her hands to her sides, fingering the fringe on the edge of her shawl. Warmth penetrated her gloves and she looked down to see Lord Ian's hand sitting next to her, his little finger almost on top of hers. She looked up into his face, but his focus remained straight ahead.

CONRAD WAS NOT sure what he was doing. His hand was almost on top of hers, but he could not bring himself to move it. If she moved hers away, he would know she did not welcome it, but as yet she had not. He felt her gaze look from their hands to his face. If he looked at her, he did not know what he would see, so he kept his focus on the vicar, though he was not hearing a single word. For all he knew, the man was announcing the return to Catholicism for all of Britain. In truth, Conrad did not think he could hear anything over the pounding of his heartbeat in his ears.

They sat that way for what seemed both an eternity and only seconds. He dared not move, worried if he did she would pull away.

Finally, Conrad took a chance and moved his little finger the rest of the way, curving it over so it intertwined with hers. He felt her breath suck in, but she did not pull away. He chanced a look at her from the corner of his eye. A small smile curved her lips, but her gaze stayed forward. Excitement pulsed in his limbs.

The people in front of them stood up and Conrad realized the vicar had ended his sermon. Jes snatched her hand back and clasped her hands together in her lap.

Lady Rachel stood up and looked at them expectantly.

Conrad smiled when he noticed Miss Standish blush at her mother's look. Lady Rachel motioned for Miss Standish to stand.

The two shared a look and Lady Rachel gave a slight shake of her head.

Conrad felt a hand on his shoulder. He turned toward the aisle and stood when he saw a large man standing next to him.

"Lord Ian? Mr. Birdwell understood ya were in the area. He is anxious to speak with ya. Come with me." His voice was low but firm.

Conrad shook his head. "I am sorry, but it will have to wait. I need to escort these ladies back to Somerstone. Perhaps..."

The man opened his coat just enough for Conrad to see the glint of a gun. "Mr. Birdwell prefers to meet now. Git someone else to see the ladies back." The man looked around the congregation.

Conrad nodded. "Allow me to make my excuses to the ladies. I will meet you in the yard."

The man shook his head and made to grab Conrad's arm.

Conrad moved back a step, almost stepping on Miss Standish's foot. He turned towards her. "Miss Standish, I am afraid I will not be able to escort you back to Somerstone. There is some business I must attend to. Please accept my apologies." He turned to find Lord Anthony or one of the Easton men to ask for their assistance, but none of them were in sight.

Only Lord Bloomsbury was in view, hovering around the Standishes like a drenched rat. Conrad looked for anyone else, but alas.... He closed his eyes, bracing himself for the reaction his next words would elicit. "Lord Bloomsbury, would you be so kind as to see the Standish ladies back to Somerstone?"

Miss Standish's eyes widened and her lips pressed into a tight line.

"Of course, my lord. I am a gentleman, after all." He put his arm out. "Come Miss Standish. I do not like to keep mother waiting and she has been standing outside for several minutes already."

Miss Standish looked over her shoulder at Conrad as she was led away, hurt, confusion and anger all warring for dominance in her gaze.

Conrad's shoulders sagged.

"Come along, *my lord*. There will always be another lady for you to seduce." He gave a throaty laugh.

The suggestion in his tone made Conrad fume. Were it not for the gun tucked at his hip, Conrad would have landed him a facer for such a remark. The man grasped Conrad by the arm, but he pulled it free and turned on the man. "Touch me again and you will see just how unpleasant I can be."

The man sneered as they passed through the doorway. "Birdwell don't want ya slipping away again." He directed Conrad to an old, worn farm wagon off to the side of the churchyard. Shoving Conrad towards the back, the man then climbed onto the bench.

Conrad shook his head. "If you think I am riding in the back of this...cart, you are daft. Move over."

The man grudgingly scooted over, allowing Conrad to ride with him. They rode in silence for a while. Finally, Conrad looked over. "How long will this journey take? I have other commitments today."

The man laughed. "I'm sure you do. I have heard tell of your *commitments*."

Conrad clenched his fists at his side. "You did not answer my question."

"Close. It'll not be long now." Not long was an understatement. It was at least another half hour before the cart finally stopped and the man pushed Conrad off the bench. "We're here."

They had passed through two other small villages before reaching their destination. Conrad looked about. It was difficult to even call this place a village. It was more like a cluster of houses with two or three establishments interspersed.

The man guided him to the entry of a shabby looking inn. As he opened the door, he gave Conrad a shove inside.

Conrad turned and glared at him. "I will not say it again. Keep your hands off of me. Do you understand?"

The man glared back. "You do not scare me, *my lord*, so there is no need to threaten me."

A portly man, with beady eyes, entered from a back room behind the tap bar. "Ah, Lord Ian. I told ya I'd find ya." He smiled to reveal yellow and brown teeth. "Now, as to the money ya own me..."

Anger surged through Conrad. It was just as he suspected. A gambling debt. Conrad took a deep breath, looking around the filthy room. From the amount of money he had been paying out for Ian's debts of late, Conrad guessed this was the only type of establishment Ian was welcome in anymore.

"I have your money, but I do not have my bank book with me. I do not usually take such things with me to church." He smirked at the innkeeper.

"All one thousand pounds?"

Conrad kept his face passive, even as his stomach dropped. Ian's debts were getting progressively larger. This had to stop. "I remember it being less. Are you trying to cheat me?" Having no idea how much the debt actually was, Conrad hoped he was not being taken for more than Ian had actually gambled.

"It was. But not by much. You can consider the extra hundred interest and a fee for having to track you down."

"The thousand will see us settled? I will never have to see your seedy face again?"

Mr. Birdwell motioned to the man in the corner. "Burns, here, will git ya to Somerstone so you can git my money. Once he brings ya back here with the money, *then* we will be square."

Conrad wanted nothing more than to boil his brother in oil. "If you think I am returning, you are dicked in the nob. You may accompany me back to Somerstone if you wish. Or I can send the note with a messenger."

"I just found you. Don't think ya are getting away from me again." He called over Mr. Burns, before boring his gaze into Conrad. "Ya aren't in a position to make demands. Burns is the one with the pistol."

Conrad clenched his teeth. "Very well. Mr. Burns let's get on with it."

8

A CHANGE IN AFFECTIONS?

"*A*re you sure you will not join the party, Mama? You have kept indoors too much. The fresh air will do wonders." Jes looked at her mother with worried eyes. "Lord Ian is sure to prove amusing."

Her mother stared, weariness evident in her eyes. "You are right, Jes. I have remained indoors for too long. The weather is beautiful, but I believe I will enjoy the grounds here today." She patted Jes on the arm, a smile coming to her face.

"Are you feeling unwell again? Did the church service tire you too much? I can remain behind if you need..."

Her mother cut her off. "Nonsense. I am well. I just do not need to go traipsing about some castle when there are so many lovely gardens here." She shooed Jes out of her bedchambers. "I am not an old woman who needs constant care. Go have fun."

Jes entered the marbled hall, tying the ribbons of her bonnet as she walked. Guests were gathering to make a trip to Wentworth Castle. It was deemed too far to walk, so the carriages would transport the large group. She looked about, hoping Lord Ian had decided to make the journey, smiling at the thought of the stories he would concoct. Spotting him on the opposite side of the room, she moved in his direction. He was speaking with his friends, laughing and making a spectacle of himself.

She approached the group, giving a small curtsy and made a show of addressing all of them, but her eyes addressed him only. "Good morning, gentlemen. Are you to make the journey to Wentworth Castle with us?"

He looked at her with a mixture of bewilderment and dismissal. "It would appear I am. Why else would I be donning my coat and hat?"

Mr. Teirny laughed loudly, while Lord Anthony and Mr. Beauchamp smiled, pity evident in their eyes.

Feeling the heat rise in her cheeks, she took a step back, confusion clouding her eyes. Lord Ian stepped away from her. "Now, if you will excuse me. I have asked to escort Miss Barton. It would be terribly rude for me to keep her waiting a moment longer."

Jes stood rooted in place. She did not know where to go or how to react. Lord Ian had never dismissed her, let alone so thoroughly. Tears began to sting at the back of her eyes. She pushed them down, determined not to make a scene. Squaring her shoulders, she walked towards the entryway. What had made him so indifferent? No, there was much more than indifference in his look. It was almost as if he did not know her and did not desire to make her acquaintance. The thought renewed the burning in her eyes.

What could she have done to change his opinion of her so quickly and drastically? He had seemed more than amiable at church. Although, his departure was abrupt and odd. Had the gentleman he left the church with said something? Perhaps he told Lord Ian about their financial situation? Jes clasped her hands, twisting at her fingers inside her gloves. Perhaps he was like his mother and had decided she was not worth his notice. Jes straightened her spine. If that was how he felt, she did not need the likes of him. She tried to swallow, but the lump made it difficult. She just needed to continue telling herself she was better off without the likes of him. Before long she would believe it. Or at least she hoped so.

Stepping onto the pebbled drive, Jes waited to be shown to a carriage. The same handsome footman from when they first arrived helped her into the next available coach. He gave her a smile, one that should have made her swoon, but it did nothing. She returned it with a quick, artificial grin. Sitting on the bench, she looked around the carriage seeing Lord Beauchamp, Mrs. Jones, and Lord Anthony shared the conveyance. Lord Anthony caught her glance and smirked at her. She forced her gaze down to the very interesting fringe at the bottom of her wrap.

"Is your mother still not well?" The question from Mrs. Jones brought Jes's head up.

"She is doing much better; thank you for inquiring. She has not yet explored the gardens at Somerstone and wished to do so today."

Her gaze drifted over to Lord Anthony, who looked at her pityingly. Turning her head to look out the window, she silently willed the coach to move faster. The conversation around her continued, but she paid it no mind. The dull ache in her chest made it difficult to keep the tears from falling. *You are a ninny, Jessica Standish. A gentleman pays you a small amount of attention and you turn into a watering pot over him.* She searched her memory for some reason Lord Ian should spurn her in such a cruel way—in such a public manner. Their lack of fortune was the only reason that came to mind. Perhaps it was not a defect in her, but in him, that caused the change.

The carriage rolled through a gated entrance and made its way around the formal pond in the middle of the drive. Statues spouted water in all directions, the droplets of water shimmering in the sun's rays. When she thought she could stand it no longer, the coach swayed to a stop. Jes kept her eyes focused out the window until the door opened and a footman began to hand them out.

Taking in a calming gulp of air, Jes looked at the house and grounds around her. While Wentworth was not nearly the size of Somerstone, it was indeed impressive. The mixture of the Baroque and Palladian styles reminded her of Somerstone, even though the homes looked entirely different.

The group walked around the main house and onto the expansive grounds. Someone must have applied to the housekeeper for permission, for a liveried footman stood at the front of the group, beginning his speech on the history of the home and grounds.

They started in one of the many formal gardens, the ha-has separating them from the carefully planned wilderness beyond. Jes tried to keep her attention on the footman and his properly rehearsed monologue as the group walked about. They stopped at the Corinthian Temple and Archer's Hill Gate, Jes could not focus. Instead, she found herself seeking out the form of Lord Ian. Was he making up stories and sharing them with Miss Barton? The thought made her stomach burn and tighten. She had come to think of the stories as a private joke between the two of them. She spotted him up ahead, speaking closely with the young lady. Miss Barton did not laugh, nor did he, but her constant blush was enough to guess the nature of their conversation.

Having convinced herself she had caught him at a bad time earlier, Jes moved up next to him as they all gazed out at the Sun Monument. "I have heard this is the exact location where Caesar surrendered to King Henry the VIII." She smiled up at him, only to have it drop from her face at his look of bewilderment.

"I believe you are mistaken, miss." He laughed mockingly. "A bluestocking you are not." He gave her one last look of disdain, before leading Miss Barton away.

Jes dropped her head, but not before seeing the look of sympathy Miss Barton cast over her shoulder. A shaky breath, slightly resembling a donkey's bray, passed her lips. Tightly twisting her fingers until they ached under her gloves. Lifting her head high, she followed the crowd, hearing nothing the footman said of the Castle folly.

"Ah, Miss Standish. How are you enjoying the tour?" Jes looked up to see Mr. Oscar Easton standing at her side. His brow wrinkled slightly as if he were concerned about something.

Pasting on a wide smile, she responded with as much cheer as she could fake. "Very well, Mr. Easton. Thank you for asking." Her gaze bounced to Lord Ian and then back. "And you? Are you enjoying the gardens?"

"Very much. The rhododendron and magnolia blooms are quite exquisite."

Jes smiled genuinely this time. "I would not have guessed you to have such an interest in flowers."

Mr. Easton pinked slightly. "Only those specific ones. They are some of my mother's favorite. She has them planted in her private garden at home."

"Ah, it is more you are a good son than a botanist." Her mood cheered slightly. As long as her gaze did not stray, she might just make it through the afternoon.

Mr. Easton nodded then put his arm out for her to take hold; together, they walked down the incline and away from the castle. She moved to let go when they reached level ground, but he placed his hand over hers, keeping it firmly in place. Jes let a small smile grace her lips, even as she wished someone else was in possession of her hand.

Conrad could barely constrain his frustration at the amount of time it had taken him to settle up with Mr. Birdwell. Why must Ian receive all the enjoyment from his escapades and Conrad suffer all the inconveniences? On his ride back to Somerstone, Conrad had had time to think about many things. He had decided, when the proper time presented itself, he would confide in Miss Standish his true identity. He had also decided to cut Ian off financially. He was singlehandedly ruining the Pinkerton family name and finances. While Conrad could do little about the damage to the family name, he could do something about the money. And he planned to do so as soon as he saw Ian again.

When Conrad finally returned to Somerstone and changed his clothes, he was informed the other guests had long since left for the excursion to the castle. Conrad's frustration mounted. This event was one of the few planned activities he had anticipated attending. He had thought of an array of very tall tales about the various follies and monuments at Wentworth, ready to share them with Miss Standish. He knew she would have laughed a great deal, something he was very disappointed to miss. Instead, he sat in his chambers writing a letter to his sister and going over the correspondence his butler had forwarded on to Somerstone. Dinner would be his first opportunity to talk with Miss Standish and it could not come fast enough.

When he entered the drawing room, he spotted her in the far corner. His heart rate picked up when he saw her and raced when her eyes met his. But it plummeted to his stomach when there was no pleasant smile or pertly arched brow in response. It was as if something had washed all the happiness from her countenance. When he moved toward her, she excused herself and walked in the opposite direction. If he did not know better, he might think she was purposely avoiding him. But that was absurd. What could possibly have happened to make her want to avoid him? He paused. Was she so angry with him for asking Bloomsbury to escort her back to Somerstone? Conrad thought she might not like the idea, but he had no notion she would stop speaking to him over it.

The butler entered and announced dinner. Miss Barton appeared at his side. "It looks as though we are paired for dinner, as well, my lord."

Conrad's brow furrowed. "As well, Miss Barton?"

"Um, yes...I mean...after we were together for the castle tour...." She stammered in nervousness.

Conrad continued to look at her in confusion. He had no idea what she was talking about. It was no wonder Miss Standish found Miss Barton tiresome. The girl had little confidence and seemed to flounder at any disagreement. She tried to make conversation with Conrad throughout the meal, but he found it difficult to pay attention. She kept speaking as if they had an intimate acquaintance.

Even more than the conversation itself, Conrad found it difficult to pay mind to anyone but Miss Standish. She was seated across the table and down several chairs from him. He caught her looking in his direction several times, but each time she would drop her head and scowl at her plate. As the meal progressed, Conrad found himself watching her more and more. On the few occasions his gaze drifted from Miss Standish he noticed Lady Rachel glaring daggers at him. What he had done to either woman he did not know. It was the longest dinner he had ever endured.

When the gentleman finally rejoined the ladies in the parlor, his eyes sought her out immediately. Her back was to the door and she was looking out the window into the darkness.

Walking to that side of the room, Conrad was intercepted by Lady Rachel. Her eyes were cold and her mouth set in a firm line.

"I do not know what your intentions are with my daughter, but I will give you a warning. There is something amiss with you. Something I do not trust. Make no mistake. I am not totally without influence. If you hurt my Jes, I will see to it you will not escape unscathed." She drew herself up to her full height. "Do I make myself clear?"

Conrad nodded, unsure what to say.

Without another word, Lady Rachel glided to the other side of the room where the matrons were gathered.

Conrad shook his head, slightly shaken by the set down. He looked over to Jes once more and decided any threat from her mother was worth the price. Sidling up next to her, he cocked his head to the side, whispering into her ear. "Good evening, Miss Standish. It is lovely to see you. How was your afternoon?"

She turned confusion and hurt evident on her face. "We are to be friends again, are we?"

His brow creased. "Friends again? Whatever are you speaking of? When have we not been friends?"

A cross between a huff and a sob escaped her lips. "Truly? We spent the afternoon exploring Wentworth Castle's grounds and you completely ignored me. It was as if you did not even know me. On the few occasions I ventured into a conversation, you brushed me aside as if I were a street urchin begging for food. That, my lord, is when I assumed we were no longer friends."

"But—" Conrad opened his mouth to refute his presence there. This was the second person asserting he was at the castle when he most certainly was not. Suddenly, the confusion turned to understanding and then anger. *Ian.* Conrad's teeth clenched until his jaw hurt. It was the only explanation. The lout had arrived. He let out a deep breath and ran his hand through his hair. A most un-Ian thing to do. His mind began to work, trying to find a way to smooth the situation over, while still coming up with several ways to destroy his brother. "I must apologize for my earlier dismissal, Miss Standish. I had just received a letter from home, with some unpleasant news. It seems my sister has taken ill. I am afraid I let it take precedence in my thoughts. Please beg pardon." She looked only slightly less hurt.

"Miss Barton certainly seemed more than a preoccupation, my lord." There was a challenge in her voice.

"Miss Barton?" Ah, now the earlier conversation made sense. "Her father and mine were chums at Eton. When I found she was to be unaccompanied on the outing, I offered merely as a favor to her father." Conrad bristled at the lies he was heaping upon his previous ones. Oh, how had he gotten himself into this position? He looked Miss Standish in the eyes, pleading. "Please, Miss Standish. You are one of the only females here I do not find simpering and intolerable." He expected a laugh but was disappointed.

Barely a crack seemed to form in her frosty demeanor. One brow arched slightly, but not in her usual pert way. "I am slightly more tolerable than the rest?" Her nostrils flared slightly. "I am merely a diversion while you are stuck here at this party?"

His face heated and his stomach soured. "No, no, no. That is not what...er, that is to say, I did not speak clearly. What I meant to say is I find you..." He stopped. What was his plan? Give her a list of everything he found appealing about her? Confess he got lost in her eyes? Or perhaps that he found her lips most tempting? Even the idea of explaining how he found her witty, intelligent and perceptive seemed far too intimate.

She cleared her throat, her hands on her very shapely hips. Conrad shook his head to clear those thoughts.

"Yes, my lord? I am anxious to hear what exactly you believe I am." A challenge appeared in her eyes, her mouth a tight white line.

This was not how he had envisioned this evening turning out.

He rubbed at his earlobe. "You are neither simpering nor intolerable, Miss Standish. I find your company most acceptable. Please accept my earlier apology, as terrible as it may have been."

The challenge seemed to drop. Her mouth relaxed into a slight smile, only with no sparkle or glow to it. He growled low in his throat. Ian was an idiot and Conrad planned to throttle him as soon as their paths crossed. When Miss Standish still did not respond, Conrad frowned. Ian was not the only idiot here. Ian may have removed her smile completely, but Conrad had done nothing so far to restore it.

She began to look around the room as if she needed to escape his presence. The thought she would follow through brought panic, his chest tightening.

He extended his arm, his eyes begging her to accept it. When she tentatively placed her hand on his forearm, he placed his over hers, squeezing lightly. "I understand there are luminaries in the garden tonight. If you would be so kind as to accompany me, perhaps you could tell me which of the sights at Wentworth Castle were your favorite."

She looked up at him, hurt still evident in her eyes. He wanted to tell her everything right then, but the quickening of his heart and the tightening in his stomach convinced him it would not fix the hurt. It would only cause more because he had been lying to her from the beginning. Telling her now would cause a scene and most assuredly ruin her reputation. Lady Rachel's warning echoed in his mind. It would be better if he found a more private moment when it was just the two of them. Perhaps he could escort her on a turn about the gardens. His brain warred with itself about the proper time and place. Was there was such a thing; a proper time to confess you are a liar?

Miss Standish cleared her throat, bringing him back to the present. His internal debate was not helping her mood.

He grasped at anything, hoping to prolong their time together. "The history at the castle is almost as interesting as this old place." He raised a brow in exaggerated excitement.

She dropped her head, her eyes fixed on the toes of her slippers. Her voice was quiet. "I confess, I did not pay much attention to the footman and his informative tour."

"Surely you heard the whole place was built because of a competition with the Du'Brevan family?" He leaned in closer, whispering the secret. "However, you most likely did not hear that it was the site of the first battle of the American Colonial Revolt."

He felt her body relax at his side, her smile twitching, even as tears hovered in her eyes. His heart ripped a little.

At last, a little laugh broke out. "I tried to point out the spot where Caesar surrendered to Henry VIII. But it seemed you were too involved with Miss Barton." Her head ducked as she quickly inhaled. Her free hand reached up and quickly wiped across her face.

He let out a laugh, but guilt stripped it of any conviction. "Drat it all! Did I miss that bit of history? Perhaps we can make another trip where we can enlighten each other." He led her to the terrace doors. "Granted, it shall never be as exciting as a spirit hunt, but little is."

They stopped at the railing, looking out over the Italian Garden. It glowed with the muted light of thousands of luminaries.

A sharp intake of breath sounded next to him. From the corner of his eye, he saw her face soften in the glowing light. "It's beautiful," she whispered.

He looked down at her, though her eyes remained on the garden. "Indeed it is." His voice was scarcely louder than a whisper.

She turned just then, catching him staring at her, but turned back quickly. When she spoke, her voice sounded slightly stran-gled. "Speaking of ghosts. Were you aware there is one haunting the grounds of the castle?"

Conrad tsked and chuckled mockingly. "I believe I would know of such a thing if it really did exist."

Those pert brows raised high, righting Conrad's world. "Ah, but there is. It is said the daughter of the earl fell in love with the gardener." She looked back out over the grounds, but he continued watching her. "The girl's parents forbade the match and she refused to marry another. They say she died of a broken heart and her lonely spirit now haunts the gardens."

She turned to face him again, the breeze picking up a lock and blowing it onto her lips. His hand lifted, tucking the hair behind her ear, his gaze never leaving her face. Her eyes drifted closed for a moment, as a breath escaped her. When she opened them and looked at him, he smiled, hoping she could see how much he meant it.

Trying for an unaffected tone, at which he failed miserably, he shrugged. "Then there is nothing for it. We must visit the castle together."

9

REUNITED BROTHERS

*C*onrad looked out his window over the garden. The door from the hallway opened, but he did not turn around. "Is it as I suspect?" he asked. "Is he here?"

Crandall walked quietly over to the window. "Yes. He arrived early this morning."

Conrad gave a mirthless laugh. "That bit of information I am very aware of. I spent most of the evening attempting to fix what he did on the castle outing." Conrad felt the muscles in his shoulders tighten. "Do you know where he is now?"

Crandall stayed quiet for a moment. When he spoke, his voice was subdued. "I believe he is in the billiards room, with Mr. Teirny."

"No doubt wagering money he does not have." Conrad clenched his teeth, feeling the pressure all the way into his neck. "What is he doing wandering about the house? Does he care nothing about the scandal this will cause if other guests should find out what we have done?"

Conrad ran a hand across the back of his neck. "Crandall, will you please find Ian and quietly inform him I wish to speak with him immediately?"

Crandall bowed to the reflection in the mirror. "I will have him here shortly, my lord."

Conrad stood firmly rooted in front of the window. What was he to do with Ian? It seemed he became more reckless with each passing year. His shoulders stooped. Where had the turning point been, the point where they had taken different paths?

The door opened and Conrad heard his brother walk in. He could identify Ian's gait anywhere. Keeping his back to him, Conrad let out a sigh. "Why did you not inform me you had arrived?"

He heard the smirk in Ian's voice. "I tried to find you, brother, but you were nowhere to be found. I sat in this room for a full hour waiting on you. When Teirny came knocking, what was I to do?"

"Make your excuses and stay put. That was the plan if you will recall." Conrad turned around, fire burning in his eyes. "I was in some nearby village. It seems a Mr. Birdwell heard you were attending this party. He sent an associate of his to collect on the debt you owe him." He glared at his brother. "That is why I could not be found."

Ian smiled. "I am relieved to hear that bit has been settled."

Conrad growled. "That is all you have to say for yourself? Do you know how much I had to pay to dismiss your debt, Ian?"

"Calm yourself, Conrad. I just had a run of bad luck. It will turn back in my favor soon."

Ian's complete lack of apology left Conrad speechless. His mouth hung slightly open.

"And now that I am here, you may remove yourself to Peny-moor. Thank you for filling in for me." Ian waved his hand in the air as if Conrad was an annoying insect buzzing about him.

Conrad shook his head. "You will not dismiss me, Ian. I will leave when I am ready." Conrad smiled at the widening of Ian's eyes. Conrad staying longer was the last thing Ian wanted. "Am I to understand an agreement has been reached between you and Miss Simmons?"

Ian waved the question aside. "Did you really believe I would offer for Miss Simmons?"

Conrad clenched his fists at his sides. "That was the reason for this charade, as you well know. You told me that was your intent. I should never have agreed to this," Conrad waved wildly about the room, "had I not believed something would come of the association."

Ian shrugged. "She would have been tolerable, I suppose." He grinned devilishly. "Or rather her money would have been. But her father caught wind of my most recent string of bad luck and forbade the match."

Scrubbing a hand over his face, Conrad didn't know which problem he should focus his anger on; there were so many to choose from. "I understand you made quite an impression on several of the guests while on the tour of the castle this morning."

Ian smiled his lazy, devil-take-care smile. Conrad wanted to punch it off his face. "Yes, I know. But Miss Barton is a bit too... naïve. She and I do not pair well together."

Breathing in through his nose, Conrad tried to gain control. "Miss Barton was not the only one to take notice of you. I believe Miss Standish was well aware of your presence. Especially after you brushed her aside as if she were a maid or something else beneath your notice."

"Miss Standish?" Ian paused and looked at the ceiling, his finger tapping his chin. "Oh, yes." He shrugged. "Actually, she is beneath my notice. I have it on good authority she is on the rocks."

Conrad shook his head at his brother. "You are one to talk. You are cucumberish yourself."

Ian's eyes widened slightly, his brows rising. "Tell me brother, why such an interest in Miss Standish and her mistreatment?"

Conrad turned away from him. "I am always concerned when you treat someone poorly. It is not Miss Standish, per se, as much as the notion of you treating any lady in such a manner."

Conrad turned at the tsk coming from behind him. "I am surprised she has caught your eye. Mother would never approve of you tipping your hat at the daughter of a merchant."

"She is more than that." Conrad shot back before he thought about the comment. "Besides, she hails from nobility."

"I see." Ian folded his arms across his chest. "So you will be arriving at the party as yourself, then?" Conrad did not miss the disappointment in Ian's voice.

"I have not decided the length of my visit nor who I shall be attending as. I have business that needs my attention soon." At the light in Ian's eye, Conrad continued. "But for the time we will be here together. I shall have Crandall arrange our schedule so neither of us is locked up here for days on end." He almost laughed at Ian's scowl. "But you must be kind to Miss Standish when you are about the house. She cannot be rebuffed at one meeting and friends at the next. Or better yet, do not be where she is. And please, avoid Lady Rachel as well."

JES TIPTOED DOWN THE HALLWAY, her candle flicking shadows on the walls. Pushing open the door to the library, she peeked inside. Her mother would surely not approve of lurking around the house in her nightrail, with only a shawl to cover her. But she was having difficulty sleeping and needed a book to occupy her thoughts.

She looked at the fireplace and smiled. What had Lord Ian

called this room—the Leather Smell room? He claimed this was the place where George Washington had first read Thomas Payne and realized he wanted to be the Prime Minister of a new country.

Jes had never considered herself a clever person, but when she was with Lord Ian, a side she had never known existed emerged. She liked that side of her and especially that side of him. Her heart stuttered when she thought of him looking at her on the balcony this evening. Had he really said she was beautiful? He could have been looking at her but been speaking of the gardens, as she was. But the look in his gaze.... People called her mother beautiful, but not Jes. She was plain in comparison.

She pulled a book on Henry VII off the shelf. Opening it, she read a few lines. *A bluestocking you are not.* The words came unbidden to her mind. This side of Lord Ian she had witnessed that morning. He was cutting and cruel then. There were two opposite sides of the gentleman's personality. One was pleasant and fun. The other—she did not know what to think about him now. It left her off balance.

She replaced the book and scanned the next set of shelves. There were several books on Somerstone and the surrounding area. Her eye caught on a book spine several shelves over. The light cover stood out amongst all of the deep burgundy, browns, and blacks.

Holding her candle high, Jes reached up and pulled it from the shelves. A shiver ran down her spine as she ran a thumb over the cover. Ghost stories from across the country. A jittery excitement tingled in her stomach. She clutched the book tightly to her, looking around the room as if expecting a ghost to appear at any moment.

She moved to the door, knowing this was not the right room to read stories such as this. But she knew the perfect spot—the third floor. Her hand trembled slightly at the thought of returning to the nursery wing, even as excitement zinged through her. Her heart thudded loudly in her ears. Would the little boy be back tonight? What would she do if she saw him while she was by herself? The last time Lord Ian had been there to grasp, but tonight she had only her book to comfort her.

She climbed the stairs, with every step her mind questioning the prudence of this course of action. But then in the next moment, she would berate herself for being a coward. And so it went until she found herself on the third-floor landing. The hallways were dark and still.

Jes glanced in both directions, but nothing appeared in the darkness. She straightened her shoulders and held the candlestick out in front of her. All of the windows in the corridor were gabled, pushing out into the roof line. Some of the bump outs held small tables, while others had seats built into them. As Jes walked by, her light filled each alcove before returning to the space in front of her as she moved past.

She whispered, mostly to herself, but also to the little boy if he happened to be near. "There is nothing to be scared about. No one is going to hurt you." Repeating it over and over helped her jumpy nerves. Her hand still shook, sending wobbly shadows over the walls of the corridor.

When she reached the doorway of the nursery, the same place the group had seen the ghost the night before, Jes placed her candle on the window seat. She looked up and down the hallway again before sitting down on the cushion. Pulling her legs up under her, she tucked her nightdress around her feet.

Her candle flickered in the breeze coming through the window frame and Jes shivered even though it was not particularly cool.

She picked up the candle and opened the book. The spine was stiff and tight as if it had not been opened much, making it difficult to hold open the book and still hold the candle. Jes remembered a small half table in the alcove before this one. Placing the candle back on the bench, she walked lightly to the next window. Ducking into the darkened area, she tried to lift the small table but was surprised by its weight. It was a sturdy piece of furniture, no doubt needed in the children's wing, but much too heavy for her to pick up and move.

Placing her fingers under the edge on either side, Jes tugged on the table, pulling it out from the wall. Scratching sounded as the legs scooted across the wooden floorboards. She winced at the noise echoing down the corridor.

Jes dropped her hands. What if she had marred the floor? She padded back to the window seat and snatched up the candle. When she held the candle down low to examine the floor around the table and no marks were visible, her breath came out in a puff and her shoulders sagged with relief.

Jes placed the candle holder on the table top and resumed pulling it the few remaining rods down the corridor. Once she reached the window seat, she pushed the table up against the wall.

The candle flickered warmly into the little alcove, making it feel less scary; cozy even. Jes tucked herself into the corner and opened the book in her lap.

A smile curved her lips upon reading the first sentence. When she had arrived at Somerstone, she would never have believed this was how she would occupy her nights—reading ghost stories by candlelight in a haunted wing of the house.

Jes read in a quiet whisper. "The Tale of the Brown Lady." She recited the tale in soft tones, reading of the lady's history and her marriage to a viscount. Gooseflesh erupted on Jes's arms when she reached the part where the lady began to haunt the halls of the Norfolk estate.

A creak of wood snapped Jes's head up and sent her heart racing. She angled her head out of the alcove, peering down the corridor, focusing her attention on the noises around her. When no other sounds reached her ears, she chided herself for her ridiculousness and turned her attention back to her book.

She had not read more than a paragraph when another noise brought her head out of the nook again. She placed the book to her side and pushing her legs to the floor, she stood up. Soft footfalls reached her ears, but nothing appeared in the darkness. The hair on her neck stood on end and her hands felt cold as she clasped them together.

This was not a good idea. Why had she thought this was the best place to read? Who in their right mind read a book on ghost stories in a haunted house hallway? No one knew she was up here. Her mind raced through several dire scenarios.

She could hear the footsteps, but in the long hallway, it was difficult to locate their source. Jes turned away from the direction of the staircase and peered into the darkness. From the dim light of the candle, she could see the little tables and chairs of the schoolroom to her right. She lifted her candle high, trying to light farther down the hall.

A hand grasped her shoulder and Jes screamed, dropping her candle to the ground. Before she could turn, the flame was stomped out by a polished black boot, at the same time a hand came across her mouth.

In the darkness, Jes felt her knees buckle. Was this the end for her?

A voice flittered into her ears, low and calm. "Do not scream. I am not here to harm you." She recognized that voice.

Jes fell back against Lord Ian, relief flooding through her. As her heartbeat began to slow, she turned towards him.

Her eyes adjusted to the light and she saw the firm set of his lips.

She stepped away from him, remembering the state of dress

she was in. Jes pulled her shawl tighter about her body, grateful for the darkness and the privacy it was providing. She let out a shaky breath. "You nearly scared the wits out of me."

He placed his hand on her upper arms, pulling her closer and scrutinizing her. "I did not mean to frighten you. Are you well?"

Jes knew she should pull away, but after her scare, she was enjoying his closeness. "Yes. I was only a little startled. What would you have done had I fainted?" Her voice held both accusation and curiosity.

His deep chuckle warmed the gooseflesh from her arms. "I always carry a small vial of smelling salts, for such an occasion." He looked her over and as if just realizing she was in her night clothes, dropped his hands to his side. "What the devil are you doing up here at this time of night?"

Jes raised her chin, her spine straightening. "I could ask the same of you?"

Lord Ian touched the tip of her nose with his finger. "Ah, but I asked first."

Jes folded her arms across her chest, making sure her shawl was covering as much as possible. Her face heated as she thought about the repercussions of her actions. "If you must know, I was reading."

Lord Ian chuckled again. It made her stomach flutter, which made her blush even more. She was glad it was dark. Surely he could not see the deepening crimson on her face.

"Perhaps you did not realize there is a library for such things. I could introduce you to it in the morning if you would like?"

"Of course I know there is a library," Jes snapped. "Where do you think I found the book?"

Lord Ian reached over and snatched the book from the cushion before she could stop him. He leaned into the window, tilting the book cover towards the small amount of light coming in from the moon. "Ghost Stories of the North Country?" Even in the darkness, she could see one of his brows quirk up. "Yes, I can see why you would wish to read this book here, in this spot."

Jes smiled. "Really?"

He shook his head. "No." Then he laughed. "I do not understand. I should think this is the last place you would want to read such a book. And especially at night." He reached out and took her chin in his thumb and forefinger.

Heat shot all the way to her toes at his touch.

He turned her head from side to side. "Odd, you appear to be sane."

She yanked her head from his hands and huffed. "I thought you—of all people..." She shook her head and snatched the book from his hands. "Oh, never you mind. Now if you will excuse me, I am feeling quite exhausted."

Lord Ian bent and picked up the candle. "Wait, I will see you to your room. You may have riled the spirits tonight. I will not sleep a wink unless I know you are safe."

Jes tried to be angry, but a grin teased the sides of her mouth. She was thrilled, even if he was jesting, that he was worried about her.

They walked the length of the hallway to the staircase. When she began to descend, he came beside her and offered his arm. "It is very dark. I do not want you to fall."

She placed her hand on his arm. "But what if you should fall and take me down with you? That would not be very gentlemanly."

She could hear the smile in his voice. "Then I suggest you keep a firm hold on that railing and save us both."

They reached the landing without mishap, which Jes had mixed feelings about. Falling in a heap with Lord Ian...she should not think of such things.

He waited for her to indicate which direction they would go. She looked over to him, barely making out his profile. "Why did you come upstairs tonight? You could not possibly have known I was there. I told no one."

Lord Ian gave her back the book and placed his hands behind his back. "I was preparing to retire when an eerie scraping sounded above my head. I know who resides there and thought I should investigate." He shrugged. "I thought it might be a fun story to regale you with at breakfast."

Her stomach flopped again. "That would have been me, moving the table to hold my candle." She stopped abruptly and turned her head back toward the stairs. "Oh, I should go back and return the table to its rightful place." Her eyes widened. "I am sure the candle left a mark on the runner."

Lord Ian put a hand on her arm. "Do not worry yourself. I will see to all of it first thing."

She turned back to face him. It may have been the lack of light, but the way he looked at her—it was the same look he had last night on the terrace. Her breath hitched. She stopped in front of the door to her chambers. "But it was my doing. You should not h...."

He put a finger to her lips. "Enough. Do not worry yourself." He pulled his hand away.

Jes looked up at him. Did he want to kiss her as much as she wanted him to? She swallowed hard. Surely such thoughts would send her straight to hell, or so the vicar in Durham had taught. Her eyes drifted to his lips and then back to his eyes.

He lifted his hands but dropped them back to his sides. Taking a deep breath, he stepped back several paces. "This is your room?"

Jes nodded.

"Then I shall leave you for now. Pleasant dreams, Miss Standish."

He turned and walked in the opposite direction.

Jes went into her room and closed the door behind her. Leaning against the door, she clutched the book to her chest. She would never have imagined her night would turn out as it did. It was so much better than even her imagination could conjure.

10

MAPS AND BILLIARDS

*J*es bolted upright in her bed, her eyes scanning the room frantically. Raising a hand to her cheek, she felt a cold dampness there. Searching the room again, she fell back onto her pillow, pulling the covers up around her neck, trying to ward off the chill suddenly creeping up her skin.

Slapping her hands down against the bed covers, she chided herself. *Jes, you are pigeon-livered!* She scowled at the ceiling. It was the second time in as many nights, she had dreamed about cold wet kisses from a non-existent ghost.

Jes let out a chuckle, shaking her head at her own absurdity. Throwing back the bed linens, she moved to the wardrobe to begin dressing for the day.

As she searched her gowns, she reviewed the daily schedule in her mind. She did not recall anything until cards after dinner.

A lavender day dress seemed the best choice. Laying it on the bed, she tugged on the bell cord, calling the maid. There were far too many buttons for Jes to manage on her own. It was times such as these when Jes missed Annie. Letting her go had been one of the harder things Jes had done after her father's creditors had been paid.

She sat at her dressing table looking at herself in the mirror. What she desired was solitude this morning. After her encounter with Lord Ian last night, she was even more confused by him. The library seemed the best place to spend her day. She would be able to keep her mind off him while immersing herself in a good novel.

Grabbing a handful of hair, she pulled her dark locks into a simple chignon at the back of her neck. It was not the most flattering look, but she had no intention of spending time with anyone who should care. Studying her reflection, she squinted back at herself. Her father's blood ran more prominently in her veins. He had been a handsome man, but it had not translated well into a female. Or so she had been told numerous times by her aunt. Her eyebrows were perhaps a bit too thick and her eyes too close together. Even her forehead seemed larger than was deemed acceptable for a female.

Turning her face, this way then that, Jes shrugged. There was nothing for it.

A light knock sounded on the door before Fanny slipped inside. "I've come to help you dress." She moved to the wardrobe and gathered all of the needed clothing. Without a word, the girl tied Jes's stays and then lifted the dress over her head. As Fanny finished fastening the last button, Jes ran her hands down the front of her dress. "Thank you."

The girl eyed the knot at the back of Jes's neck. "Can I dress up your hair a bit, miss?"

Jes shook her head. "No, Fanny. It is fine the way it is. I do not plan to leave the library, although I will need your assistance in dressing for dinner."

"Of course, miss." Fanny picked up the nightgown lying in a pile on the floor, and straightened the bed covers.

"That can wait for later, Fanny. For now, could you please have a breakfast tray delivered to the library?"

Fanny nodded and curtsied as Jes walked into the hallway.

She pushed open the library door, peering inside to assure she was alone. Moving to the shelves, she found the section she was looking for. Her fingers ran along each spine, the feel of the imprinted leather calming her. She read each title, her mouth moving with each word.

After going through several cases, Jes had yet to find something which appealed to her. She turned her back to the shelves and gazed about the room, not knowing what exactly she was looking for until she spotted a table to one side. It contained several long flat drawers. With a slight tug, the top drawer opened, exposing several maps. Pulling out the first one, she studied it closely. Her chest constricted as her finger followed the coastline of the continent. Her eyes burned as memories flooded over her. A tear spilled onto her cheek.

A slight breeze fluttered the edge of the map as the library door pushed open. Jes looked up, expecting to see Fanny and her breakfast tray. Her stomach dropped to her toes when instead she saw Lord Ian carrying the tray. Her heart skittered. It seemed her body could not decide if it was happy or disappointed at his arrival.

He smiled. "I found your maid loading this tray with breakfast. After much coaxing, she finally confided in me where you were hiding." He set the tray on a table on the opposite side of the room and looked about the room. "I have found myself missing the library at Penymoor. Would I be imposing too much if I asked to join you?"

Jes's brow furrowed as she stared at the tray. He was to be amiable today. Her objective had been to have a day free of all things pertaining to Lord Ian, most particularly the man himself.

His face seemed to fall, as he watched her nod her head. "I see. Well, I am sorry to have imposed on your solitude." He bowed politely. "Miss Standish," He said in farewell. In four long, quick strides, he reached the door.

When he reached for the handle, Jes heard herself call out to him. "Wait."

He stopped, turning slowly around. His gaze never left her eyes as he walked cautiously towards her. When he got closer, his face crinkled in concern. "Have you been crying?"

She ducked her head. First, she practically begged him to stay with her and now he knew she had been crying. He must think her utterly ridiculous.

He stepped closer, the smell of sandalwood and soap wafting forward with the movement, overtaking all of her senses. Slowly and quietly she inhaled deeply, her eyes closing as her nerves crackled like the fire in the grate.

When she opened her eyes, she did not know where to look. She was not prepared to look at him yet, so she stared down at her slippers. Her brain was going in a thousand different directions; part of her wanted him closer, while another wanted him to leave altogether.

He tipped up her chin with his finger. She thought for a moment her heart had stopped until it thundered so loudly she was convinced he could hear it also. All thought fled from her brain.

She looked into his eyes and her breath caught in her throat at the intensity she saw there.

"Why have you been crying?" His voice was soft and kind,

which made it harder to swallow and force a breath out. She stared at him for a moment and then she looked at the table and map.

He followed her gaze with his own. His hand dropped to the small of her back, moving with her to the table. He looked from the maps to her with curiosity. "Reading maps made you cry? Is it the coloring the cartographer used, or perhaps the penmanship is not to your liking?"

Her lips parted as she looked up at him in confusion. His smile fell away for the second time in a matter of minutes. "I am sorry, I did not mean to make light of whatever was troubling you. I have never been very good at handling a crying woman. My sister says I am utterly useless."

A chuckle managed to push past the lump in her throat. It was enough to bring a half smile back to his lips.

"Although I do find the colors on this map a bit garish, they were not the cause of my tears," Jes finally managed to say.

He turned towards the map. Placing a hand on the table, he leaned over it. "I see nothing else objectionable enough to warrant such a strong reaction."

Jes ran her finger along the coastline again. "My father was a tradesman. He had a fleet of ships, sailing in all directions in search of goods to bring back to England. He always traveled on *The Lady Rachel*. He claimed it made for better prices if he could haggle for them himself." She smiled at the memory. "Whenever he returned from a journey, he would pull out our map and trace the journey with my finger, telling me stories about every stop he made." Her finger stopped on the outline of Spain, tears pricking at her eyes again.

Lord Ian placed his hand on top of hers, tracing the outlines of Italy, Greece and the Ottoman Empire. Her breath hitched, as the heat from his arm seeped through the thin fabric of her sleeves.

"Is your father away now? Is that why you are sad?" His breath lifted the hairs along her neck.

She shook her head. "No. His ship was caught in a storm. It was lost, along with the rest of his fleet. That was almost two years ago."

Their fingers stopped. He looked down at their hands and then up to her face—his eyes full of emotion. She could see sadness and grief, but there was more. Something else she could not understand.

He sighed, running a hand through his hair. "Lud. I am sorry to have made light of such a situation. You must think me a complete cad."

Her hand felt immediately cold at his removal. "No!" She grabbed at his arm, both of their eyes drawn there. Pulling her hand away, she continued as heat colored her cheeks. "You could not have known the cause. Please do not chastise yourself unduly."

He moved away, collecting two chairs and setting them down at the table. "Would you tell me about some of his adventures?"

Her stomach flopped and her heart nearly burst out of her chest.

This was the type of man she could love. She swallowed hard. Did love? Everything she had believed was love, up to this point, seemed false and shallow when compared to what she felt right now. She squinted at him as she allowed the thought to settle in her mind.

———

Conrad smiled as he strode down the hallway, his nerves tingling with excitement and joy. He had spent a perfectly delightful morning scouring maps of Europe and India with Miss Standish. Who would have thought hearing about someone else's journeys could prove so entertaining? They were so immersed in their conversation, she had completely forgotten about her breakfast until it had grown cold.

When she had finally excused herself to have tea with her mother, Conrad had wanted to tie her to a chair and lock the door, so he could spend more time with her. Thankfully, he was not prone to the outlandish. But now he was left restless, with nothing to do. Having already been on his morning ride, he roamed the halls in hopes of finding something to occupy his time until the evening's entertainments began.

The sound of ivory hitting ivory drew his attention. Following the sounds, he found himself outside the billiards room. Courtenay and Lord Felling were in the midst of a game. Conrad leaned against the door frame, watching the two play. Felling moved into position, his stick lined up with the ball when he stopped and stood.

"Kendal? What are you doing here? I had no idea you were to attend this party also."

Conrad opened his mouth, but Courtenay spoke first.

"That is not Kendal, it is his brother, Lord Ian." There was caution in his voice.

Felling walked over, eying Conrad closely. "I beg to disagree. This is Lord Kendal as sure as my father is the Duke of Somerset."

Both men now stood in front of him, scrutinizing every freckle and line. Finally, Conrad could bear it no longer. "Take a step back, the both of you."

Courtenay raised a brow. "Well?"

Sighing, Conrad nodded his head. Felling laughed, smacking him on the back, while Courtenay just stood there, shaking his head.

"Has it been you the whole time?"

Conrad shrugged.

"Why did you not tell me from the beginning, Kendal? There is much we need to discuss before the season begins."

"Do you know the scandal this will cause if it ever gets out? Both Ian and I would be severely censured. And neither of us can afford that, although for entirely different reasons. So please, continue calling me Lord Ian, as much as it makes my skin crawl."

Felling laughed loudly. "I am sorry I have missed watching this performance."

Conrad scowled. "You do not know the half of it. The cad arrived yesterday and did not even make me aware of his presence." A growl crawled from his throat. "While I was settling one of his most recent gambling debts, he was touring a nearby castle, making life unbearable for some of the more respectable guests."

Courtenay smiled. "I can guess which guest you are speaking of. Oscar mentioned something about your odd behavior on the outing. I should have put it together."

The remark earned Courtenay a glower. "And then, after I spent the evening making amends for his boorish behavior, he had the audacity to laugh and excuse me from the party entirely!" His body shook with anger at the memory of Miss Standish's cold reception. "I have had it with him. I will no longer be funding his carefree lifestyle. My father would turn in his grave to see what Ian has become."

Courtenay shot Conrad a sympathetic grimace, while Lord Felling clapped him on the back.

Taking a deep breath, Conrad gestured to the billiard table. "Well, now you both know who I am, we have much to discuss."

Courtenay looked towards the door. "It is too risky to discuss here. Too many prying eyes and ears."

Conrad nodded. "It may be best to wait until after the party."

Felling moved back to the billiard table, lining up his shot. "I will admit, I am relieved to find you here. I was becoming concerned about the lack of information coming from you."

Conrad pulled a cue from the rack, confident in his work toward social reform. He rolled his shoulders. It was about the only thing he felt confident in right now. "You have nothing to worry about. Everyone will be lined up when it comes time for the vote."

11

THE LAST DANCE

*C*onrad stepped into the parlor, searching the room until his gaze landed on Miss Standish. His shoulders relaxed and his face softened at the sight of her. She sat near the fire with Miss Townshend, Miss Anne, and Miss Fairchild smiling and laughing. Her whole face radiated joy. Conrad stood to the side, observing her. He had come to realize last night that he cared for her. If he let himself consider it, he might even say—he stopped short of admitting that much. Although watching her now, he surrendered to the idea that he could watch her for the rest of his life.

She was elegant in an unrehearsed and natural way. He knew of many ladies who practiced such moves, with less effective results.

He was relieved to see Ian had stayed true to his word and kept to his room for the evening. The last thing Conrad needed was Ian coming down and making a muddle of everything, just because he was too impatient to wait for his turn to socialize.

Conrad noticed Miss Townshend stand and move in the direction of Lord Anthony. Conrad raised a brow. He was not sure what a lady could find appealing about the man, but he could not be unhappy about it as it freed up a seat near Miss Standish. He walked the length of the room, stopping at the chair across from her.

"Is this seat taken, ladies?" He glanced at Miss Fairchild, trying to include her, but his eyes quickly returned to Miss Standish.

His heart hammered when she smiled up at him. Only yesterday he had been convinced she would never look at him that way again.

"It is not taken, my lord. At least not yet." Was that hope in her eyes?

Miss Fairchild nodded her consent, then turned her attention to her sketchbook and Miss Anne.

Conrad sat down, stretching out his legs and crossing them at his ankles. He looked around the room, his gaze coming back to rest on Miss Standish. Motioning with his head in the direction of the card tables, he asked. "It seems cards are the entertainment for tonight. Would you care for a game of whist?" He secretly hoped she would decline, for Conrad found cards a tedious waste of time. But if it meant he could sit across from Miss Standish and observe her unabashedly, then perhaps he could take up a hand.

Miss Standish shrugged. "I am content to watch unless you would like to play?"

He waved her question aside. "I am not overly fond of cards."

They picked up their conversation from the library, continuing almost as if there had been no interruption. "If you could visit one country, which would it be?" He sat up, leaning forward, his elbows on his knees.

Without hesitation, she blurted, "Egypt."

A brow quirked upward. "Really, Miss Standish? Pray, tell?"

She clasped her hands in her lap. "Oh, apart from the pyramids and remnants of the great pharaohs, there was also a magnificent library." She lifted a delicate shoulder. "I realize it is no longer there, but just being in the same spot it once was...it would be incredible. The knowledge that was housed...." She looked up at him through her lashes, a smile dancing on the edge of her lips. "Besides, in Egypt, your stories may actually ring true."

Conrad opened his mouth to reply but was cut short by a ruckus at one of the card tables.

Conrad raised his brows, standing to get a better look. When Miss Standish glanced from the card table to him, he held out his hand to help her out of her seat.

They moved toward the table, watching with the rest of the room as Courtenay and Miss Graystock challenged Miss Easton and Sir James. A wager had been placed on the outcome of the current hand. From Conrad's vantage point, it did not appear Miss Easton was trying very hard to win. When the last card was played and victory declared to Courtenay and Miss Graystock, Conrad patted him on the back.

"Pray, what was the wager?"

Courtenay laughed raising a brow at Miss Easton. "A dance. More precisely, a waltz."

As if on cue, the servants began to move the furniture and roll up the rugs. Conrad thumped Courtenay on the back again, knowing his own excitement and eagerness was surely apparent. But he did not care. Courtenay only had eyes for Miss Easton, anyhow.

Conrad turned to Miss Standish and bowed. "May I claim the waltz, Miss Standish." If the glow in her eyes was any indication, she was just as excited as he.

She dipped a curtsy. "It would be a pleasure, my lord."

His hand slid around her waist and he pulled her closer to him. She felt tentative at first, keeping a polite distance between them, but as the music sounded from the pianoforte and they began to move around the floor, he felt her relax. He tightened his hold, drawing her into him. Her breath caught, but she allowed him to decrease the space between them. His heart raced. Neither of them seemed willing to break their gaze and the spell they were under.

Conrad could feel the warmth of her skin, working its way up his hand and into his arm. At some point in the dance, he pulled her so close he need only drop his head and his lips could be on hers. He lowered his head a fraction, waiting to see if she would meet him halfway, or flee altogether. While she didn't close the gap entirely, she leaned further into him. His heart felt like it would beat out of his chest when he dropped his head the last few inches. Just as their breath began to mingle, the music stopped and applause broke out around them.

Miss Standish jerked back, putting more than polite space between them.

His heart dropped to his toes as he saw her cheeks color. She stared at him, a look in her eyes he had never before seen, and he yearned to know her well enough to understand it.

"W-w-would you care for another dance? It looks as though a reel will be next." He barely recognized his choked voice.

Miss Standish put a hand to her cheeks. "I think I will sit the next one out. I would like to check on my mother."

Conrad felt his face fall, disappointment washing over him. Had she not enjoyed the dance? Had he read too much into her look and taken liberties he should not have? But when she smiled, his worries evaporated like water on a hot stone walkway.

He led her over to the group of matrons sitting to the side watching the dancing. Several cast him a disapproving look. "I will fetch some refreshments and return shortly." He bowed to Lady

Rachel and all of the matrons, but his smile was directed at Miss Standish.

He was uncomfortable with the recent scowls he had been receiving from the older women at the party. Even a few of the younger ones had ceased smiling at him. It seemed one set disapproved of him being Ian and the other was unhappy he was not acting enough like Ian.

As he walked to the table a footman approached him and bowed. "A letter was just delivered for you, my lord." He handed the small folded parchment to Conrad, before turning and quitting the room.

Conrad stared down at the paper addressed to his brother. He did not recognize the hand and was at a loss as to who it was from. An uneasy pit formed in his stomach. Moving out of the crowded room, he found the Statuary Hall empty. He sunk down at the base of the statue of Jason and the Golden Fleece and cracked open the wax seal. It was from Miss Partridge, his sister's governess. At least it was not another demand for payment. She must have been informed of the situation because she addressed Conrad by name in the note. He sat up straight, his heart pounding harder with every word he read. Jane's cough had worsened and she was now delirious with fever. Miss Partridge was writing to request his immediate return.

Conrad shot to his feet, pacing like a caged lion in the Tower Menagerie. He hated to leave Miss Standish, but he needed to return home to his sister. The pull of family won out and Conrad raced to his chambers. He found Ian in the adjoining sitting room, playing a game of patience on the writing desk.

"We need to leave immediately. Jane has taken ill and is delirious with fever." Conrad moved to the bell pull, tugging on it several times. He turned back to see Ian had not so much as lifted his eyes from his game. Conrad walked over to him and swatted him across the arm. "Get up, Ian. I said we need to leave."

Ian lifted lazy eyes to Conrad. "And why should I go? I have only just arrived. It is not as if I am a doctor and can provide any measure of help." He laid a card down on his desk. "I would be better served to stay here."

Conrad grunted. "I should have known you would think only of yourself." He stomped to the shared door. "Send Keaton in to help me pack. Everyone believes Crandall is your valet so it seems he must stay with you until the party is over."

Ian finally abandoned his cards and stood up. "But, Crandall is so conservative. He knows nothing of the most current knots. My cravat will be a disaster."

Conrad stared at his brother with an open mouth. The man was beyond the pale. He cared for no one but himself. Conrad shook his head. "If you insist on staying on, will you make yourself useful and be kind to Miss Standish? I do not have time to explain things to her before I leave...." He ran a hand through his hair. "That is far too long of a conversation."

"Do you plan on returning?" Ian smiled. "I could explain it to her."

"No!" Conrad nearly leaped toward his brother. "That is the last thing I wish you to do. I do not know what I plan to do. That will depend a great deal on Jane. But I will explain to Miss Standish—somehow."

Keaton entered Ian's room. "Yes, my lord?"

Ian sighed dramatically. "My brother is leaving tonight, which means you will need to leave with him. Everyone here believes Crandall is my valet, so he will need to stay and continue in that role."

Keaton looked from one brother to the other. "Yes, my lord."

He moved into the bedchamber and began to pack up Conrad's trunks. "How soon until we depart, my lord?"

"As soon as we can. It is quite urgent."

Keaton nodded and set to work.

"It seems there is no reason for me to stay in my room for the rest of the night." Ian grabbed his tailcoat from off the chair and shrugged into it. "Send Jane my love, Conrad," Ian called over his shoulder as he left the room.

An uneasy feeling settled in Conrad's stomach for the second time. This may very well be the end of his acquaintance with Miss Standish for, after this, she would surely never speak to him again.

———

Jes and her mother sat just outside the French doors, on the terrace. Most of the couples had abandoned the area in favor of the dancing taking place inside. She looked about, ensuring they would not be overheard. "Oh, Mama! From the first time I saw Lord Ian at the Medford's ball, I believed myself in love."

Lady Rachel frowned slightly. "Jes..."

Pressing a hand on top of her mother's, Jes continued. "But since spending this last week with him, I know those early feelings were the imaginings of a foolish young girl." She closed her eyes, reveling in the memories. "My feelings run far deeper than before. When he looks at me, I feel as though I am the most beautiful creature he has ever seen. When we speak, he values my opinion and listens to what I say. I still feel those same feelings I did in the beginning, but it is so much more now."

Her mother's smile was reserved. She placed a hand on her daughter's cheek. "Oh, dearest. Just be careful. There is something about Lord Ian I do not trust."

Jes laughed nervously. Her mother voiced the same concerns

as Jes had herself. "He explained that Mama. He had received news his sister was ill. He was preoccupied, that is all. It was a singular event." She had told herself over and over there was no more to it. But when she thought on it, a sick feeling settled in her stomach. Her mother did not look completely convinced, but she offered a small smile.

Jes looked around. Lord Ian had gone to fetch some refreshment and she was surprised he was not back yet.

"I believe I have had enough fresh air. Will you be joining me inside?"

Jes shook her head.

Her mother stood. Placing a hand on Jes's shoulder, she gave it a gentle squeeze. "I am sure you are correct about Lord Ian, Jes, but take heed not to push aside the troubling aspect of his character because you think yourself...." Her mother darted a glance around the area. "Well, you understand what I am about. I do not wish to see you hurt."

Jes nodded her head, the elation of moments ago gone. She watched her mother walk back into the house, both happy and disappointed to be alone with her thoughts.

She waited on the terrace for Lord Ian to return. It was a beautiful night and she could not bring herself to return to the stuffy confines of the parlor. Guests came and went, each time sending her heart jumping, but there was no sign of him. Finally, when the lights began to dim in the parlor, Jes stood and moved towards the doors, only then realizing the evening had come to an end with no sign of Lord Ian.

The same sick feeling burned in her stomach. Why had he not returned? The afternoon at the castle came unbidden to her mind. Perhaps he had found the company of Miss Barton more to his liking tonight. But the images of him placing his hand over hers as they traced the maps made her heart thump. How could he be so atten-tive and kind in one moment and then in the next, abandon her? It was like he was two different people. Two very different people.

Jes shook her head and made her way to her bedchambers. She walked down the corridor, lost in her thoughts when a giggle brought her head up. Lord Ian stood outside Miss Summer's room, the two engaged in an intimate moment. A cry caught in Jes's throat. She clamped her mouth shut, casting her eyes down again. Her emotions threatened to explode right in front of him. The two barely registered her presence so engaged they were in each other. She rushed past them, flinging the door of her chambers open. Once the door was securely closed, Jes sank back against the solid wood.

The squelched cry started in her chest. Just as it was about to break free, Fanny appeared from the shadows. "Are you ready to prepare for bed, miss?"

Taking a stuttering breath, Jes nodded. Her throat ached for want of releasing the emotions she had stifled yet again. She sat in the dressing table chair, closing her eyes as Fanny removed the pins holding her hair in place. She tried reliving the waltz they had shared only a few hours ago. Her heart hammered against her ribs as she thought about him holding her. Throughout the dance, he had seemed to pull her closer and closer. His eyes searched hers as if he were looking for the answer to some unasked question hovering between them. She had wanted to ask him what she saw, but he was so focused and intense, she had faltered at the last minute and kept her mouth shut. Now the moment was lost forever.

She had convinced herself he was about to kiss her when the music ended. But now, after hours of waiting for him to return, and then witnessing him participating in the act with another lady,

Jes felt like a fool. She was now unsure of everything she felt where Lord Ian was concerned.

There had been a moment of disappointment when she declined another dance. Perhaps that is why he had sought another partner and forgotten all about her. Or maybe he had been trying to tell her there was no interest on his part. Perhaps that was what she was unable to read in his eyes.

When Fanny finally shut the door behind her, Jes slipped into bed, closing her eyes in the darkness. Tears spilled from the corner of her eyes. Running down her nose, they would hang there for a moment before dropping onto her pillow. Taking in slow, deliberate breaths, Jes returned to the memory of the waltz. It seemed that was all she was to have, after all.

DISCOVERING UNHAPPY TRUTHS

*J*es stepped down from the carriage, looking about the small village. Lord Ian was already halfway up the road, a young lady on each arm. Her stomach twisted, the pang of jealousy tightening her throat. She pushed it down. Was she not the one he had chosen for the waltz?

He had been polite to her this morning, but nothing beyond formalities. He must be trying to allay any rumors by spending time with the other young ladies. Jes had begun to hear the whispers, implying there was an attachment forming. She frowned. The thought did not sit well. She had been delighted by the insinuations. But what of him? Did he care about rumors linking them together? Was he embarrassed by her? She had, while not in so many words, told him of her family's financial difficulties. Perhaps, given the time to consider, he had decided she was not worthy of his attention.

Her frown deepened and she began to twist at the ends of her bonnet ribbons.

Miss Barton walked alongside Jes, placing a hand on her arm.

"Miss Standish, I believe a new bonnet is just what I need. Come join me in the milliner's shop."

Jes allowed herself to be pulled along, spending what felt like hours among the ribbons and bows. They finally left the shop, with several new bonnets for Miss Barton.

As they walked down the street, Jes looked at the storefronts, wondering which shop Lord Ian had gone into and if the ladies were still with him. Her heart squeezed in her chest.

She spotted a bookstore down the way. Her heart was heavy and in need of peace. It was just the shop she needed. Jes tugged Miss Barton in that direction, but she pulled back.

"I thought we should peek in the sweet shop. I have not had a peppermint in ages."

Jes nodded towards the shop. "I would prefer to look in the bookshop."

Miss Barton grimaced. "Why would you want to look at a bunch of dusty old books?"

The need to visit the shop became almost too much for Jes to bear. She gave Miss Barton a smile. "Perhaps we should separate and meet up later for tea? I shall meet you in thirty minutes."

Without waiting for a response, Jes removed Miss Barton's hand and stepped off the walkway to cross the street.

The smell of leather and parchment greeted Jes as she pushed the door open and entered the shop. With her eyes closed, she turned in a slow circle, soaking in the sunlight filtering through the windows. A calm began to envelop her, easing the tension in her shoulders and working its way down her body. Her mind quieted.

When she opened her eyes, an old man with a slightly hunched back stared at her through thick spectacles. A smile curved his lips, creasing his wrinkled face even more. "I feel the same way, every time I come into the shop. Is there something I can help you find?"

Jes shook her head, regret lacing her words. "I will only be looking today, thank you." She moved to the shelves, her fingers reverently rubbing over each book. Oh, how she wished she had some pin money to spend on one. She looked down at the dress she wore, irritated at what it must have cost. The funds would have been so much better spent in a shop such as this. A sigh escaped. There was no sense dwelling on things long past.

Her fingers stilled on a book. Pulling it out she smiled at the front cover. It was a history of Somerstone Manor and the Du'Breven family. Jes opened the book, looking first at the pictures of the Hounds-Coat and Painted Drawing Rooms. A chuckle escaped as she remembered Lord Ian calling the latter the Yellow Room. Looking at page after page, she thought back on that day, a warmth settling in her chest. It was the first time she had spent much time with him, outside of a ballroom.

"Are you sure you would not like to purchase the book, miss?"

Jes shook her head. "I am sorry, but not today." The clock on the wall gave a single chime. Had it really already been thirty minutes? She replaced the book. "I must be going. Thank you for allowing me to look about."

As she placed her hand on the doorknob, Lord Ian walked down the opposite sidewalk. Jes stood still, watching as he stopped at the doorway of a drab looking inn. He looked both ways, before pushing open the door and entering.

Jes stepped out onto the sidewalk, mimicking Lord Ian as she also looked both ways, hoping not to encounter an acquaintance. She crossed the street. Walking past the inn, she tried to subtly peek in through the windows. Now she was closer, she could faintly see several tables filled with men hunched over. Obviously, this was not just an inn. Lord Ian sat at one of the middle tables, a woman sitting very close to him, her arm about his neck, her fingers twirling in his hair. He reached for a glass of deep amber liquid, draining it in a single swallow.

Jes stepped back in shock. She continued walking, her brow furrowed. Was Lord Ian a gambler? The notion did not seem correct. At the card game the previous night, he had claimed he was uninterested in cards. He even raised his brows when he learned of the wager. Was he purposely trying to mislead her? Was he not interested last night because there was no money to be won? And what of the woman next to him? She looked to be—Jes swallowed the bile pushing its way upward. No, he would never be with such a woman. Would he?

An alley ran alongside the inn. Jes ducked into its shadow. She needed to think or be sick; she wasn't sure which would take precedence. Finding a pile of crates, she sat down. What was she to do?

Anger suddenly reared up inside of her. How dare he use her as a distraction. Had he led her to believe he cared for her on purpose or had she interpreted it incorrectly?

If she sat on the far edge of the crate, she could just make out the doorway to the inn. She would wait for the scoundrel and inform him of her newly formed low opinion. The decision eased the sting of her wounded pride, but, the ache in her chest only intensified.

She smoothed her skirts over her legs, pulling her reticule closer to her body. Looking at it, she changed her mind and tucked it behind her back. Then she leaned against the wall and waited.

A gentle, cooling breeze blew through the alleyway and her eyes began to droop. The restless sleep from the night before made it difficult to stay awake. Before long she drifted to sleep.

A crash brought her eyes open wide. She frantically looked about, trying to figure out where she was. Suddenly she remembered, her stomach clenching in fear. What had she been thinking? Falling asleep, alone in a darkened alley? She shook at the thoughts of what could have befallen her.

She noticed the alley was not the only place lacking in sunlight. Another crash sounded in the distance. Thunder. The heavens looked as if they would open up before she could make it to the carriage. The carriages! Panic nearly choked her as she saw the spaces empty. They had returned to the manor without her.

Jes dropped her head into her hands. No, no, no! This could not be happening. Had no one missed her? Not that they would have known where to look for her if they had tried.

She took a fortifying breath and squared her shoulders as she began to walk. It could not be more than three or four miles back to Somerstone. She could make it on foot. It was not so very far. Huffing and muttering under her breath, her frustration grew with every step she took. She was mad at her mother for dragging her to this blasted house party—yes, she thought it, even though her mother would surely disapprove of a lady using such a word. She was mad at Lord Ian for confusing her so completely and making her lose sleep. Just last night, she had told her mother she loved him. How could she love a man such as this? A wastrel. A gambler.

A stilted sigh escaped her lips. Most of all, she was angry at herself. She was the one who had put herself in her current situation. As if mocking her stupidity, the heavens opened up and the rain began to fall.

Immediately, she was soaked to the skin. Even her bonnet could not protect her from the rain pelting down. Her hair stuck to her face and neck, as water ran down her cheeks. Mud caked her half boots and coated the hem of her gown. She stood rooted to her spot, no longer caring about being wet and dirty. Tears fell and mixed with the raindrops coursing down her cheeks.

Horse hooves pounding in the distance brought her head up sharply. She looked about for a place to hide and found nothing but wide, open fields. She immediately added that to her ever-growing list of complaints.

Holding her head up high, she kept walking, ignoring the horse and rider as they came to a stop in front of her.

"Miss Standish? Is that you?"

Jes looked up through the rain, seeing Lady Du'Breven's footman peering down at her. She nodded her head, hoping he did not notice the redness of her eyes. It seemed all she did, of late, was cry. Another grievance to add to the list.

He leaned over, putting out a hand to help her up. "Your mother was concerned when you did not return with the carriages. I was sent to look for you." He looked up at the sky. "I should have brought a carriage, but the storm did not seem so imminent when I left. I apologize, but this will have to do."

Jes placed her foot in the stirrup, trying to help him pull her up. With very little effort, she was seated to his front. It was difficult to put the proper distance between them sitting sidesaddle, but she scooted as far forward as possible. Then she turned back just enough to offer him a smile. "Thank you for coming for me."

He tipped his head, water running off his hat brim and onto her arm. "It is always my pleasure to help a beautiful lady."

Jes nodded, despair settling in her chest. As she was fast discovering, men are never truthful in the things they say to a lady.

———

CONRAD HAD TRAVELED throughout the night. He found he was able to keep thoughts of Miss Standish at bay, as long as he pushed to go faster. But now, in the light of day, he finally stopped long enough to rest his horse and his weary body. He entered the inn, ready to secure a room and rest his eyes for a few hours. He leaned against the bar, waiting for the innkeeper to help him. He sighed, tapping his thumb on the bar top.

"Kendal? Is that you?"

Conrad looked around the room. Standing in the doorway of a private parlor stood the Duke of Shearsby. Conrad smiled. Shearsby was one of his dearest friends. He had liked the duke from their first meeting at Brooks several years before. The gentleman had an easy way about him, with a smile always at the ready.

Shearsby stepped forward, clasping one of Conrad's hands while thumping him on the back with the other. "How are you doing? Look you dreadful, man. What are you doing in Hellifield Pele?"

"I am just passing through on my way back to Penymoor from South Yorkshire. What of you, Shearsby? This is certainly not Leicestershire." Conrad rubbed at his eyes.

The duke guided Conrad over to their table and motioned to the servant. Shearsby sat Conrad down in a chair. "What were you doing in Yorkshire?"

"Your Grace." Conrad smiled and kissed the duchess on the cheek. He motioned for her to retake her seat. "I was at a house party when I received word that Jane was ill and suffering from a fever. I set out immediately for Westmorland." Conrad put his elbows on his knees, dropping his head into his hands.

The duke chuckled, taking the seat between his wife and Conrad. "Did I hear you correctly, Kendal? You were at a house party?"

Conrad raised his head and smirked. "Indeed, you did. A guest of the infamous Countess Du'Breven."

"I have never met the woman. I only know her by reputation—but it is quite a reputation." The duke raised a brow. "I am surprised. I thought you abhorred all things society. A house party

119

is the ton at its worst. What could possibly have enticed you to attend such an event?"

Conrad shook his head. "It was all Ian's plan. He was to attend but was otherwise engaged trying to secure Miss Simmons' hand. He convinced me to attend in his stead until he could come himself." Looking back, Conrad could see how silly the plan was. He should have known Ian would never actually offer for a woman. Conrad ran a hand over the back of his neck. "It was a complete disaster. Thankfully, he arrived in enough time for me to leave when Miss Partridge wrote to hasten my return."

Shearsby shook his head as if trying to understand. "You were attending the party as your brother?" His brows rose high on his head. "I do not know your brother well, but I believe I know enough to be disappointed to have missed the charade. I am certain it would have been most amusing." His eyes danced with mirth.

Conrad scowled. "Yes, it was a difficult role to play. Especially when our visits overlapped by a day or two. As I said, I was most happy to leave him to the crowd, while I quietly went on my way." His chest tightened as he thought back to Miss Standish. She had been the bright spot of the trip into Yorkshire. More than just a bright spot. He pushed the thoughts away. They only brought on disappointment in himself and resentment towards his brother.

The duchess's voice pulled him back to the dining table.

"Excuse me, Your Grace? I must have been wool-gathering." Conrad grimaced.

The duke smiled widely, making Conrad only scowl more.

She spoke again. "I thought we agreed on Christian names, my lord."

Conrad bowed his head. "My apologies, Violet."

She smiled. "Certainly, Conrad, there was something redeeming about the party. Was there nothing there for you to

"Besides, we both know you do not wish to return to Nottinghamshire. I know what it must be like to be under Aunt Lydia's thumb."

"Lydia has been very kind to us." Lady Rachel raised a shaky hand to her cheek. "What do you wish me to say, Tad?"

His voice was soft. "Say you will be joining us at Morley Park upon quitting this house party."

Jes held her breath and bit her lower lip. Her stomach twisted into knots. It was as if her entire future balanced on the edge of a cliff, ready to crash to the earth with one shake of her mother's head.

Lady Rachel squared her shoulders and nodded twice. "I always loved the dower house when I was a girl."

Jes and the duke both exhaled at the same time—great whooshes of air—causing laughter to fill the room. While Jes was relieved, she was also a bit befuddled. How was such generosity to be repaid?

A maid brought a tea tray into the room. The duchess inclined her head, indicating Lady Rachel could pour out. The ladies began to chat as the tension in the air began to clear. Jes leaned closer to her cousin. "Thank you, Tad. It is more than most relations would do."

The duke winked at her. "We are closer than most relations. As I said, I think of you as a sister. I only wish I could have found you sooner."

Her thoughts returned to his earlier conversation and confusion knit her brow. "Who did you say informed you of our whereabouts? I do not believe I caught the person's name."

A sly smile turned the corners of her cousin's mouth. "You did not hear it because I did not say." Jes opened her mouth to speak, but he cut her off. "And I gave my word I would not speak the gentleman's name. So please, Jes, do not ask again." The sparkle in his eye brought a smile to her lips, even as she narrowed her eyes at him. "But I can assure you, he is a great admirer of the lovely Miss Standish."

Heat warmed her cheeks at the notion she could have a secret admirer. But as they moved into polite conversation, the question continued to nag at her. The earlier relief she had felt tempered as new questions of a mysterious gentleman filled her head. She thought back on the other guests, unable to recall anyone leaving the party early. She looked up at Tad once more, her mouth open in question.

He raised a brow and gave a slight shake of his head. Jes knew she would get no answers from him, but she also knew she would not be able to let it go.

CONRAD RUBBED the wax stick in a circular motion over the folds in the parchment. He removed the signet ring from his small finger and pressed it into the red puddle, before placing it on top of a stack on the corner of his desk. He stood and moved to the bell pull.

"Yes, my lord?" His butler had a way of appearing without a sound and in record time.

Conrad held up the letter. "Please send this with a messenger immediately. I need a response as soon as possible."

Frampton took the missive and bowed. "Yes, my lord."

Conrad stretched side to side, trying to work out a few kinks from his neck and back. By the time he had arrived home last evening, the fever powders had successfully cooled Jane's brow. She still had a cough, but her color was good and her spirits were improved. Conrad looked around his study. With Jane not needing his attention, there was little else to do.

It was lulls such as this when his thoughts drifted to Miss Standish. She was never far away, waiting in the back of his mind, constantly occupying his dreams. What was she doing today? Had she planned to go on any outings? If so, where would they visit and would she make up fictional stories with someone else? Possibly even Ian? His stomach burned at the thought.

He grunted in dissatisfaction. A distraction was needed. Perhaps the library could offer some diversion. He had been meaning to employ a different means of organizing the shelves—a task he had intended to set a maid to work on, but given his current state of mind, Conrad decided to begin the enormous undertaking on his own. Leaving his study, he made his way down the hall. When he entered, he set right to work pulling an armload of books off the shelf and carrying them over to the table.

Turning back toward the shelf, he was stopped when his gaze caught sight of something sticking out of a drawer on the table. Walking over, he pulled it open so as to push the offending parchment back inside, when a map caught his eye. It was almost identical to the one he had examined with Miss Standish at Somerstone. Without thinking, he pulled it out. Pushing the books to one side, he laid the map on the table. His finger traced the coastline as his eyes closed. He could smell the lavender always surrounding her as if she stood next to him.

A growl sounded in his throat, his hands fisted at his side. This was not the room to vanquish her memory. While she had never been in his home, he did not think he would ever see a library that did not conjure her memory. He sighed. It was a pity, for he very much enjoyed the library. Or rather he had. He ran an agitated hand through his hair. Would he ever be able to think on her without a degree of tightness in his chest and churning in his stomach? At this moment, it seemed an impossible task.

FALSE ATTRACTIONS AND
DEMANDING MISSIVES

*J*es entered the breakfast room. Her lips pressed tightly together, as Lord Ian and Mr. Teirny both stood to greet her. Word of her dowry had not taken long to spread throughout the group. She had no idea how or where it started. All she knew was by the end of dinner the previous evening, whisperings of her new wealth circulated among most of the social circles at the party. She was surprised to receive almost smothering attention from several of the men—Mr. Teirny and Lord Ian being the most persistent.

"May I get you a plate, Miss Standish?" Mr. Teirny was quick to ask. "You look perfectly lovely this morning."

Shaking her head, she replied through clenched teeth. "No thank you, sir." Did they really think her such a dolt? Think she could not see through the false charm?

She moved around him to the sideboard. Picking up a plate, she selected several items before turning toward the breakfast table.

Her plate was plucked from her hands. "Please, Miss Standish.

I have saved a seat for you next to me." Lord Ian deposited her breakfast at an empty spot and pulled out a chair, motioning for her to sit.

She tightened her hands into fists at her side, deciding she actually preferred Lord Bloomsbury to either of these two men. Both were making a spectacle of themselves and in turn, of her. Lord Ian was one of the last people she wished to be seated near.

Especially when Mr. Oscar Easton sat several seats down the table and on the opposite side. He quirked a smile, his shoulder raising slightly.

"Did you rest well, Miss Standish? Judging from your radiant glow I would guess the answer to be yes." Lord Ian said, tucking the chair under her.

She placed a few bites in her mouth before glancing over at him, barely recognizing the man. He seemed to be a chameleon, changing his personality to whatever situation came along. She was unable to even muster a smile. The more he spoke, the angrier she became. How had she ever thought her heart yearned for this man? Granted, his behavior now was more calculated and transparent than it had been during the house tour or even in the library. Had she missed these obvious cues or had they not been on display then?

She stuffed a large bite of food into her mouth, trying to smile in spite of her bulging cheeks. Chewing a few times, she swallowed several painful gulps and pushed back her chair. "I believe I am done. If you will excuse me."

Before either man could unseat themselves, she quickly walked from the room, stepping around the corner and out of the view of the guests still eating. She had not missed the raised brows and darting glances of the other guests. Leaning against the wall she closed her eyes, trying to get back her shattered sense of peace. While her cousin surely thought he was doing her a favor by providing the dowry, she had serious doubts as to the prudence of the gift. Since her arrival, she had shifted from the fortune hunter to the hunted. She placed a hand about her stomach as guilt burned. How could she resent such an act of kindness? Lord Ian was not the only one showing his less desirable side.

A hand snaked around the back of her waist, forcing her eyes wide open. Lord Ian placed his other hand on the wall just above her shoulder, trapping her where she stood.

"I knew you would be waiting for me." He leaned closer, his breath brushing against her neck. Was that alcohol she smelled?

Her eyes watered and heat burned on her cheeks. Shoving him hard, his shock allowed her to duck under his arm and move beyond his reach. Hurrying down the corridor, she turned back suddenly. "Keep your distance, my lord." His title was spit from her mouth. Picking up her skirts, she rushed the rest the way to the library.

She pushed open the door, leaning against it once it was closed.

A pinch tightened her chest when she glanced at the table where the maps were kept. She told herself Lord Ian had been a fake and a fraud at every encounter, but a few of their interactions left her unable to fully convince herself of that fact. The time spent in this room with him was one she could not quite reconcile. She stomped her foot and moved further into the library, angry with herself for harboring tender feelings for this room—for that man. He had seemed so sincere speaking about her father. And his touch.... Her breath slowly squeezed from her throat. How could he have touched her with such affinity and not mean it? He had seemed as affected by the contact as she.

Her spine stiffened. But it was all a lie.

The door squeaked open on its hinges. Jes spun around, ready to flee.

Mr. Oscar Easton poked his head in the door. "Ah, Miss Standish. Your mother thought I might find you here."

Jes pretended to look at a shelf of books. She could not have him realize she was mooning over some memory. Especially when it was now tainted by spurious motives.

When she did not reply, Mr. Easton when on. "I was hoping we might work together in the poetry reading tonight." He rocked back and forth on his heels. "Unless, of course, you are already partnered."

Jes took a long deep breath before turning around and giving him a wide smile. Too wide—he surely knew something was amiss. "No, I am not yet paired with anyone." She looked at the gentleman. He was handsome, although not as striking as Lord Ian. While her heart had never thumped rapidly in her chest at the mere thought of Mr. Easton, nor did a thousand butterflies take flight in her stomach at his glance, he had never been anything but kind to her. And he had been, even before news of her dowry had circulated. Yes, Mr. Easton was a friend. Why then did that thought not make her genuinely smile?

"I would be happy to be paired with you, sir. Thank you for seeking me out." She looked to the shelves. "I believe I saw poetry in this area." The two began searching the shelves. Finally, she let out a satisfied grunt. "Ah, here they are. Now, which poet are you most partial to?"

Mr. Easton shrugged. "I will leave the decision to you. I am sure you are well versed in poetry." He raised a brow. "Or, more so than I."

Jes turned back to the shelf. Keats, Wordsworth... Lord Byron? Most definitely not. None seemed appropriate for the evening's entertainment. Alexander Pope? She pulled the book out, thumbing through its pages. Nothing caught her eye. Perhaps Coleridge? She looked up at Mr. Easton through her lashes. Could she be happy with him? Not that he had indicated any partiality on his part, but if he did, would she accept him?

The door opened and Lord Easton stepped into the room. His brow furrowed. "Oscar, what are you doing in here?"

"Miss Standish and I have been paired for the poetry reading this evening. We were trying to settle on a poem."

With narrowed eyes, Lord Easton looked at Mr. Easton. "Very well. Have you seen Tabby? I cannot find her anywhere."

Mr. Easton shook his head. "I haven't seen her this morning."

Lord Easton turned and left the library, muttering about Lord Courtenay and Miss Easton and someone being strangled.

Shrugging, Mr. Easton returned his gaze to the book in her hand, motioning with his head. "Have you decided, then?"

Jes fingered the cover. It seemed a hopeless matter. Every poem she read felt too focused on love and romance. Neither of which she wanted to be reminded about. She shelved the Pope book and looked to Mr. Easton. "What if we did a dramatic reading of a scene from Shakespeare? Perhaps A Midsummer Night's Dream?" She cringed at her cowardice. But Mr. Easton nodded his agreement.

"If that is what you wish."

What did she wish? She did not know anymore. A melancholy settled over her. This man was so kind and yet she felt at a loss to reciprocate. The indifference she felt for him, for everyone here, made her loathe Lord Ian all the more.

———————

CONRAD SLAPPED his gloves in his hand as he walked back to the house from the stables. He had been out riding more than usual since his return from Somerstone. In point of fact, his horse had never been exercised so thoroughly. He had never been riding with

Miss Standish, leaving it as one of the few pleasures left him which did not conjure her face in his mind. He looked up at the house. How she had imposed herself into nearly every room in his home was beyond him. Books, maps, even the folly on the north hillside could not be viewed without remembering some bit of conversation they had shared.

"Thunder and turf," he muttered as he walked through the door. Frampton did not even raise a brow, as if he were so accustomed to Conrad spouting such base language. A grunt sounded in Conrad's throat. Of late, such phrases were more common than he cared to admit.

He handed off his hat and gloves to the man. "Did the messenger return yet?" He knew it was too soon, but he felt compelled to ask anyway.

"No, my lord. Although, I do not expect him for several days yet."

Conrad scowled. "I will be in my study, Frampton."

"Very good, my lord."

He had not even taken a seat when the door opened and the butler entered offering a brief bow. "I am sorry to disturb you, my lord, but this just arrived by messenger. The man indicated it was of some urgency." Frampton held out a small folded parchment.

Conrad took it, examining the seal as he dismissed the man. He had seen the imprint before, but could not place from where. Cracking the seal as he sat down, he unfolded the letter, his eyes dropping to the signature at the bottom. Ah, he should have remembered the Countess's mark. What Lady Du'Breven could possibly want with him, he could not say.

The note was quite short. He skimmed over the pleasantries included in all correspondence, finally getting to the reason for the note.

I am writing to demand you get your mangy carcass back to

Yorkshire at once. A certain young lady has become quite the diamond in the eyes of your brother and Mr. Teirny upon learning of her rather substantial dowry. Though I cannot say their attention is as welcome as it would be coming from someone more...suited to her. I will expect you back before the ball.

Conrad's brow crinkled as he reread the letter, amusement and irritation battling for prominence. The Countess demanded he return? A guffaw escaped his lips. Few people dared demand anything of him. However, the Countess was not like other people.

At first, he had believed she must be speaking of Miss Standish, but he knew—she had hinted to it herself—not only did she not have a great dowry, she had no dowry at all. According to Shearsby, after paying off her husband's creditors, Lady Rachel was cleaned out.

But why should the Countess call on Conrad for the sake of another young lady? It was not as if he had paid anyone else special attention.

While the Countess tried to feign ignorance, Conrad knew she was up to her neck in machination of the romantic nature.

It bothered him he had been so obvious in his affections for Miss Standish that the Countess had taken note, but he was also intrigued that Lady Du'Breven believed Miss Standish to be displeased with Ian's attentions—if he interpreted the note correctly. The thought made Conrad pause. He was displeased with Ian's intentions toward Miss Standish, but could it be possible Miss Standish was not pleased with them either?

He sat back in his seat, his breathing becoming tight and his heart jumping erratically in his chest. Was it even possible she could have feelings for him after being left with Ian? He shook his head. Was there any chance she would overlook his dishonesty once she discovered who he really was? Conrad was a Marquess, after all. The thought did not help his mood. He wanted Miss Standish to love him, not his title.

He believed he knew Miss Standish well enough to know she did not care about titles. He ran his fingers through his hair. What was he to do? If his assumptions were correct and she could love him, he must return to Yorkshire immediately.

He shot to his feet. But what if he was wrong? What if she did, in fact, prefer Ian? Was that possible? Conrad's shoulder sagged. What woman didn't prefer Ian to Conrad? What if he opens his heart to her and she rejects him? Slowly he sat back in his chair, staring straight ahead but seeing nothing.

He needed to ride; to clear his head and make an educated decision. Standing quickly, he moved towards the door. If he let his heart decide he would be gallivanting across the countryside on his way to Somerstone with no plan or idea as to how to proceed. But he was not one to fly off in haste—he was practical.

A picture of Miss Standish and Mr. Teirny entered his mind. The man was unscrupulous.

"Fiend seize it! I cannot leave her to that viper."

In four long strides, he was across the room and striding down the hallway. "Frampton," he hollered.

The man appeared immediately. "My lord?"

"Tell Keaton to pack my bags and be ready to depart within the hour. We are going to Yorkshire. I have a ball to attend." And a lady to court, he added to himself as he climbed the stairs to his sister's bedchamber. His mind began to compile a list of problems with this plan, but he pushed them back. Instead, images of Jes— her body pulled close to his, her face tilted up towards him as he spun her around the dance floor—settled in his thoughts. Practicality fled, his decision was made. He had to try and make her his.

AN UNWELCOMED RETURN

*J*es felt smothered. The air inside the house was stale and muggy, the walls closed in on her. She had been roaming the house for nearly a quarter hour trying to find something to occupy her mind. Unfortunately, Mr. Teirny or Lord Ian seemed to find her wherever she went. Now she found herself in the hallway outside the nursery.

Memories from that night crashed over her. Her hand went to her earlobe as she remembered Lord Ian's warm breath when the ghost had appeared. Jes sagged against the wall, as the air sucked from her lungs. How could she stand to stay here until the ball? Every room, every view, every part of this estate held memories she wanted so badly to forget.

She looked out the window as she passed by on her way to the stairs, a sigh raising then dropping her shoulders. The leaves on the branches of a tree outside fluttered in the breeze. She needed that wind—needed to feel it pick up her curls and carry them away from her cheeks. She needed to feel it dance across her skin and tease the hairs on her arms and neck; to smell the lavender and honeysuckle wafting through the gardens.

Her decision made, Jes returned to her room and collected her bonnet and short gloves. She reached for her spencer, but changed her mind and left it hanging in the wardrobe.

Heading for the staircase, she bumped into Miss Graystock at the first landing. The lady looked positively forlorn since Sir James had departed.

"You look as if you are in need of some air. Come, Miss Graystock and join me for a walk." Jes pushed her own melancholy aside for the moment. It was not as if it was doing her much good, anyway. "There is a little path to the rear of the gardens. It looks very diverting." She hoped the young woman would come along, but if not, Jes intended to make the journey on her own. The thought of doing anything without certain gentlemen following along behind her, pretending to be besotted fools, was inviting.

A relieved sort of smile softened Miss Graystock's features. "That would be lovely, Miss Standish. Let me fetch my bonnet and gloves. I will meet you in the Statuary Hall."

Jes waited, observing the statues without much interest. The ball was only two days away and then she and her mother could quit this place for good and return to the estate of her cousin.

Thoughts of Morley Park brought feelings of peace. Even though her mother had been raised on the grand estate, Jes had not seen the place until after her uncle's death only five years prior. But since her cousin had become a duke, they had been invited several times. He had also made the journey to Hartlepool—something neither her uncle nor grandfather had ever done. Jes adored Tad and Violet. Yes, living at Morley Park would be wonderful.

Miss Graystock entered the room, tying the ribbons of her bonnet under her chin. "I am ready. Shall we be on our way?"

They went through a set of French doors, leading out to the

terrace. Once down the stairs, they moved towards the back of the formal gardens, leaving the estate grounds through a discrete hole in the hedgerow. A narrow animal trail serpentined up a small hill a dozen or so rods ahead. The two began to climb, slipping slightly in the mud. A breeze took hold of the loose tendrils at the back of Jes' neck, sweeping them back and forth. She stopped in her tracks, breathing in deeply, allowing her soul to be renewed.

Miss Graystock turned back. "Did you change your mind about a walk? Is the path too muddy?"

Jes shook her head. "Oh, no. I am only enjoying the crispness of the air. Let's continue."

The path ran between two rock fence lines, both green with moss. In some spots, it was grassy while others were thick with mud. Puddles pooled in the tracks of the most recent cattle to have wandered along the trail. They tried to step around the water but only succeeded in creating new ruts as their boots sunk into the wet earth.

Miss Graystock wrinkled her nose. "It does not appear we will come away from this walk without a fair amount of mud on our hemlines."

Jes pulled her left boot out, making a great sucking sound as it broke free. "Yes, and our dresses are not the only thing to suffer." A smile stretched across her face as she looked over at Miss Graystock. "If you prefer to turn back, I understand." Jes did not know the young lady well. Miss Graystock and Miss Townsend had seemed to form a ready friendship, while Jes had spent more time with Lord Ian in the beginning. She glowered at the mud. A lot of good that had done her.

"I am not afraid of a little mud, Miss Standish."

Jes smiled at her. "Then we are of one mind. The gardener indicated there is an interesting rock formation just at the top of this hill."

A set of stone steps sat before them, grass and moss growing between each stone. At the top, the trail split into two. The first was interrupted by a gate, while the other side continued on and followed along another rock wall. They followed the second path and before long came to the top where it leveled off onto a plain. A flat, grassy area lay below them to one side and to the other, Somerstone Village was visible in the distance. Jes turned in a circle, her arms stretched out to her side. She wished she had her paints. It would be difficult to get them up here, but the views would make the effort worthwhile.

Miss Graystock came up beside her. "This is magnificent." She placed a hand on Jes's arm and gave it a light squeeze. "Thank you for asking me to join you. It is just what I needed today."

Dozens of huge boulders were scattered about the ground as if God had dropped them from Heaven. Jes laughed as she scampered from formation to formation. Wind and rain had battered several of the rocks causing them to be worn at the bottoms, appearing as though the large rocks were perched precariously on top of the head of a pin. Jes squinted, cautiously putting a hand out, wanting to touch it. She pulled her hand back at the last minute, afraid it would topple over at the slightest touch.

They were all so incredible, so different, but yet the same. She came to a flat rock with half a dozen deep indentations along the top. Water from the rain had filled each one making tiny little ponds in the boulder. Jes ran her hand along it, her fingers dropping into the water and then popping back out again.

Her hand stilled as his voice came into her mind. *This is called the Lord's Rock Garden. It is famous because Spartacus and Alexander the Great signed the Treaty of Westphalia right on this very spot.*

Jes stomped her foot. Now she was hearing Lord Ian say things he had never said.

Miss Graystock came up beside her again, her brow creased. "I did not even know this place was here. Do you know what it is called?"

Jes took in a deep breath. While she did not like his voice intruding into her thoughts, she had to admit the name was appropriate. "Heaven's Rock Garden—or that is what it should be titled. I do not believe I was told the actual name."

Miss Graystock looked about. "How do you suppose these stones came to be here?"

"I don't know. Perhaps it is as the boulders at Stonehenge. They just appeared and no one knows for sure how it happened."

Miss Graystock lightly touched one of the rocks. "Do you believe they have magical powers as well? Not that I believe such nonsense."

Jes gave a quiet laugh, shaking her head. "It is a lovely thought, though. Is it not?"

They wandered about the plateau until reluctantly, Jes moved towards the path leading back to Somerstone Manor, a heavy sigh indicating her regret. "We should be getting back. I am sure you have duties for the Countess to attend to, as I am sure my mother will be getting anxious over me."

Miss Graystock joined her at the trail. "I think the way down may be more difficult. Be careful to watch your footing. I am sure it is very slippery."

Jes took one last look at the plain. She had hoped to find someplace which would not conjure memories of Lord Ian. But it was not to be. He had invaded this haven, as well. If only he had been cruel from the beginning, she could be done with him entirely. But he hadn't. He had been sweet and kind and funny. Whether those moments had been false or not, she was finding it difficult to rid herself of them. And it was those sentiments that continued to break her heart.

CONRAD HAD NEARLY FINISHED his second all-night ride in less than a week. It was no wonder his body felt tense and sore. On this ride he had not even stopped to rest his horse, pushing both of them to exhaustion. He slowed Bard to a trot. Leaning back slightly, he pulled one leg up and rested it over the saddle horn. Twisting from side to side, he stretched out his back and neck muscles. He was still several miles from Somerstone, but he was close enough to take it easy the rest of the way. Dismounting, he allowed the reins to hang slack, giving Bard a chance to graze along the roadside. Conrad didn't mind the slower pace, happy to stretch his legs for a moment.

The sound of women's laughter floated on the breeze, making it difficult to pinpoint the direction. He looked around, until he spotted two of them, walking slowly down a set of stone steps. Conrad smiled at the obvious enjoyment they were sharing. He watched them absently from beneath a crop of trees. By the time they reached the bottom of the steps, they were not too far off. One of the women turned in his direction and he recognized Miss Graystock, Lady Du'Breven's companion. She did not appear to notice him—most likely because he was hidden in the shadows.

The other woman turned and his chest tightened as he recognized Miss Standish. The graceful lines of her neck and the elegant way she walked was not something he would forget. She stepped off the last step and her foot slipped on the muddy trail. Her arms swung around wildly, as she tried to regain her balance.

Miss Graystock reached out to help but only succeeded in losing her balance as well. Both women fell into the mud, sliding several feet down the path.

Conrad dropped the reins in a panic, running from beneath the branches straight up the hillside, stopping just a few feet shy of

Miss Standish as she came to a stop. Her head was down, looking at her mud caked gloves. A laugh broke free as she shook her hands, sending bits of mud flying in all directions.

Miss Graystock gasped as a glop of mud stuck to her cheek. Then she too began to laugh.

Conrad reached a hand forward, "May I help you up, miss?"

Miss Graystock looked up first, her brow furrowed in question.

Miss Standish looked up as well, an irritated grunt escaping from her mouth. Her eyes were wide, her lips parted. She struggled to stand, refusing his hand. Conrad reached forward, grasping her arms and pulling her to her feet. "Je...Miss Standish. Are you alright?" His voice came out rushed and strained. He had not anticipated seeing her so soon upon his arrival. Indeed, he had hoped to be introduced to her as himself and then begin the task of trying to explain the truth.

The daggers in her eyes as she pushed away from him, caught him by surprise. "I did not ask for your help, my lord, and you need not volunteer it."

Unable to bear the contempt he saw there, he turned his attention to Miss Graystock. "I beg your pardon, Miss Graystock. You are well?"

She nodded her head, her gaze darting between the two of them. Her brow knit in concern.

He returned his scrutiny to Miss Standish, disappointed to see her demeanor had not changed. If anything it had grown stormier. Taking a step back, he grasped his hands behind his back, even as he yearned to reach out for her. Apparently, the Countess had understated the situation. Miss Standish did not appear to have even a spark of affection for Ian. The contrary seemed more accurate. He would have smiled at the notion had he not been afraid she would slap it right off his face. However, it was wiped away on its own once he realized when he told her the truth, she would likely look at him as she did now. His earlier delusions that she would forgive him all his lies now seemed naïve.

He offered his arm to both women, hoping to ease the tension suddenly surrounding them.

Miss Graystock took it, but Miss Standish moved down the trail. The mud kept her from progressing too quickly. Her feet fell heavy and angry, her head held high.

Conrad and Miss Graystock fell in step behind her.

Miss Standish had only gone four or five rods when her foot slipped again. Instinctively, Conrad reached out a hand to steady her. She jerked her arm out of his grasp and whirled around to face him.

"I believe I have made myself clear on several occasions, my lord. Please leave me alone and do not ever touch me again." She turned on her heel and sloshed down the path, mud splattering up the back of her dress each time her foot dropped onto the path. Surely, hell itself would part to let her pass today.

Miss Graystock kept her eyes focused on the ground in front of her.

His chest tightened and his stomach turned sour. He moved his hand up, rubbing the back of his neck. He did not know what had happened, but it was painfully obvious he needed to speak with his brother. What could he possibly have done to warrant such a reaction? There was only one possibility Conrad could think of...but no, Ian wouldn't. He was a lot of things, but certainly would not be so brazen as to force himself on a lady. Miss Standish in particular.

They reached the grassy part of the trail, which only made Miss Standish increase her pace until she reached the bottom of the path. There she halted, with her back to him, waiting for Miss Graystock to join her.

Conrad released Miss Graystock and offered a small bow. "I

believe the path is safe now. If you will excuse me, I should see to my horse." He walked only a few steps before he stopped and watched Miss Graystock work her way down the trail.

He was torn somewhere between anger and confusion. Taking a halting breath, he chastised himself. How had he gotten himself into this position? The woman he loved—for he knew it was more than affection he felt for her—hated him. Or rather, who she thought he was. And if the fire in her eyes was any indication, it was a deep, loathing hatred. How was such a thing to be overcome? Would the truth be enough or would it simply fuel the fire burning within her? A lump formed in his throat which he was unable to swallow away.

Miss Standish turned suddenly. Her brows raised. "Don't you mean Mr. Teirny's horse? I understand he won the wager."

Conrad ran a hand through his hair. This was getting better and better. If the accusation was true, which Conrad didn't doubt but it was, this was the third horse Ian had gambled away this year. And the year was not yet half over.

He gave her a sad smile. "As you say, Miss Standish. I would be in a great deal of trouble if I should lose him when he is no longer mine." He bowed to each of them. "Ladies."

Miss Graystock curtsied. "Lord Ian." She took hold of Miss Standish's arm and they continued on through an opening in the hedgerow, where they both disappeared from view.

Conrad walked back, finding Bard grazing under the trees where he had left him. Taking up the reins, Conrad mounted and headed for the stables. He allowed his anger towards his brother to build, not sure he could stand the weight of his disappointment at her reaction to him.

He was in need of fresh clothes before he presented himself to Lady Du'Breven. If the Fates were on his side, he would run into his brother before meeting with her. Conrad clenched his hands into fists as he thought about what he wanted to do to Ian. Bard slowed and tossed his head a few times in response. Loosening his hold, he clicked his tongue, setting the horse back into a canter. He and Ian had a great many things to discuss, the least of which was what the devil had he done to lose his horse?

16

DISCOVERED

*C*onrad tugged at his earlobe. He had scoured the entire estate looking for Ian, but he remained holed up somewhere unbeknown to Conrad. Most likely some local gambling hell, or worse. Ian had not even slept in his chambers. Conrad felt like an outlaw slinking around the house, hiding in dark corners whenever he spotted anyone about. He had been searching since he arrived yesterday—even taking his meals in Ian chambers, but he could not put off announcing himself to Lady Du'Breven any longer.

The time had come and he found himself outside her private sitting room. Breakfast churned in his stomach. Why was he nervous to meet with this woman? She was only a dowager countess—not the Queen mum.

He was anxious because she knew. She knew he was a besotted fool and was the only person, besides himself and Ian, who knew what an utter mess Conrad had made of this whole situation.

He took a deep breath and straightened his waistcoat before knocking on the door.

Her lady's maid opened the door and showed him into the room. She curtsied then left.

The Countess raised her eyes from the book in her lap, looking at him over the spectacles perched on her nose. "Ah, Lord..." She paused, her brows arched in question. "Kendal?"

He grinned at her. "It is a pleasure to be here, at last, my lady. I am sorry business kept me away until now." He moved closer to her and dropped his voice. "I have witnessed what a mistake that has turned out to be."

She removed her spectacles and patted his arm with her wrinkled hand. "It seems things have progressed most unhappily in the last few days. I believe you have a very difficult task ahead of you, my lord." She said the last with a touch of pity in her eyes. "While I adore your brother—I know he is a scoundrel and a spendthrift, but he has never been anything but charming to me—he has made a muddle of things."

Conrad took a deep breath, the weariness settling on his shoulders. "Yes, it appeared so when I happened upon Miss Standish during her walk with Miss Graystock yesterday."

The Countess scowled at him, her lips pulled into a tight line. "And yet, you are just now coming to see me." When Conrad offered nothing more than a shrug, she gave a quiet grunt. "Yes, Miss Graystock told me of the meeting. At the time, she also believed you to be Lord Ian."

"It is just as well. I would prefer to explain to Miss Standish myself, once I have been properly introduced to her."

"I shall see to it the introductions are made before dinner tonight." She put her glasses back on, turning her eyes back to her book. She glanced up when Conrad did not move.

He took a deep breath. "I wish you wouldn't...at least not yet. I need to speak with my brother before I make my presence common knowledge." He rubbed a hand along his neck. "And then I hope I may get a chance to explain things to Miss Standish."

"I hope you have fortitude, Kendal. She will not be easily placated." She removed her glasses again, tapping them against her lip. "Tell me, my lord. Are you above begging?"

Conrad squirmed under her scrutinizing gaze. "I had hoped it would not come to that...but I will if that is what it takes."

"I am confident you will be required to do a fair amount of pleading." She placed her glasses back on her nose and returned her attention to her book.

Conrad recognized a dismissal when he saw one, but he needed to ask. "Have you seen Ian of late? Do you know where I could find him? I have yet to discover his whereabouts."

A slight huff escaped her lips, but she did not look up. "I do not take notice of the comings and goings of each of my guests, Lord Kendal. You are a resourceful man; I am sure you will locate him."

Conrad offered a bow, feeling as if he had just been rebuked by his governess. "Thank you, my lady."

CONRAD TRIED NOT to swear under his breath. He was tired of taking all of his meals in his chambers. Who would have guessed in a house this large it would be so difficult to avoid people?

It was late afternoon and still, he had no notion where Ian could be. Conrad slinked about the halls of Somerstone hoping to discover Ian or at the very least find somewhere to hide out. Conrad turned down a hallway, a faint memory surfacing of finding Courtenay and Felling playing billiards in the room to the right. Peeking his head into the room, he found it quiet and empty.

This seemed an unlikely spot for Miss Standish to happen upon him.

He moved to the sticks sitting in the corner and selected one. Placing the balls in formation on the table, he moved to the opposite end and lined up the shot. His cue hit the balls forcefully, sending them scattering crazily around the table. He needed to rein in his emotions or he would jump the balls off the table.

A sigh slipped from his lips. It did feel good to hit something, even if it was not who he actually wished to pummel. He lined up his next shot and sent the ball flying to the end of the table where it hit the side and bounced, dropping to the floor. Laughter drew his attention from the runaway ball.

Ian stood just inside the doorway, a smirk on his face. "You have returned? Why the devil did you come back? And with only two days remaining on the invitation? You do realize the ball is tomorrow, do you not?"

Conrad straightened to his full height, his hand fisting at his side. His relationship with Ian had been strained since their father's death, but never had it reached the point of fisticuffs. After today, that claim might not be true. "I was informed you were in need of rescuing from your own folly. Is it true? Do you not even have a horse to ride once you quit this house?" Conrad turned back to the table, afraid of what he might do to Ian.

"It is only temporary."

Conrad did not need to see his brother to know he had shrugged the question off. "Until I put out for another, you mean?" Conrad smacked the ball with renewed force. "It will not be happening. Not this time. When I told you I was done paying your debts and making excuses for you, I meant it. I will not spend a single farthing on your behalf."

"Oh?" Ian scowled. "And how do you suppose I will get home?"

He moved forward, placing his hands on the edge of the billiard table.

"I do not care if you have to ride on the same saddle as Mr. Teirny or one of your other useless friends. Perhaps if you walked back to Penymoor you would realize the mess you have made of your life." Conrad took a deep breath. "Father would be...." He shook his head and moved to the other side of the table.

"Did you really travel all this way to lecture me, Conrad?" A hard edge entered Ian's voice. "If you can no longer offer me financial assistance, perhaps it is time I told Miss Standish the truth."

Conrad's eyes flicked from the table to Ian before focusing on the ball in front of him.

"Come, brother. I know the real reason for your return. What, did you learn of her dowry and decide she was good enough for you now?"

Conrad pushed past him, leaning over to line up his next shot. If he stopped, he was likely to beat his brother with the cue. "I have no notion of what you are talking about. Miss Standish has no dowry. She told me so, herself." The balls crashed against the side of the table. "Although, I find I agree with what she requested of you."

Ian quirked one brow up.

"Stay away from her."

Ian barked out a chuckle. "Oh? You have spoken with the chit, then? She has become quite high in the instep, has she not?"

Conrad straightened, placing the butt of the stick on the floor between his feet. He stared at his brother until Ian began to squirm. Shaking his head, Conrad turned away, his voice low. "I do not understand you. You have been given everything you desire and you appreciate none of it. I think it best if you experience life from the other side. Perhaps then you will realize what you had and tossed away as though it were rubbish." Conrad leaned back over the table. "As for telling Miss Standish, I already have plans to tell her myself, as soon as we are through here. Did you think I wished to continue pretending to be you?"

Ian stood still for a moment. His mouth opened then closed without uttering a word. His eyes narrowed and his nostrils flared. "You think yourself so far above me. The grand Marquess of Kendal and I just the lowly dependent brother. I do not need you or your money, my lord." He turned on his heel and ran directly into Miss Standish in the corridor.

———

COMING in from the side gardens, Jes had stopped outside the billiard room when she heard loud, terse voices from within. She saw a gentleman with his back to her, the other was leaned over the table, lining up his shot. Caring little about the dispute, Jes was just turning to leave when one of them charged through the door, nearly knocking her to the floor. Regaining her balance, she looked up into the face of Lord Ian. She scowled as her gazed flicked toward Mr. Teirny in the room.

But it wasn't Mr. Teirny staring back at her. It was another Lord Ian.

Jes glanced from one to the other, trying to understand what she was seeing. They looked exactly the same, right down to the freckle under their right eye. Although, their hair was parted on different sides. Her brow furrowed.

The gentleman who had just plowed into her backed up a few steps, then threw his head back and laughed. "Talk of the devil."

Jes gasped at the curse.

The other Lord Ian groaned and muttered, "Bad form."

His voice held a tone she recognized and suddenly all the

pieces fell into place. She turned towards the man standing behind the billiard table. "You are twins."

The one behind her snorted. "I thought you said she was clever, brother. Personally, I have never seen proof if it."

She felt the heat rise in her cheeks. It seemed two men had been pretending to be the same man. It became clear one of these men had been on the ghost hunt and in the library with her, while the other must have been at the castle. Jes swallowed hard. It was not difficult to know which one was which.

The man behind the table moved around, standing closer to her than was comfortable. She took a few steps to the side but was still able to look up into his light green eyes. Her stomach rolled as she recognized them. They were the eyes she had seen on the house tour—full of excitement and humor. They were the eyes which looked on her with so much compassion in the library. And the eyes which held so much passion after dancing the waltz with her.

She just did not know which name went with which gentleman. Had it been Lord Kendal twirling her around the dance floor or Lord Ian?

"One of you must be Lord Kendal and the other Lord Ian." She looked up into the face of the man next to her, his brow creased and tense.

He prodded at the toe of his boot with the end of his stick, before he finally looked into her eyes. He bowed deeply, but she suspected it was more to avoid her gaze than out of politeness. "Conrad Pinkerton, Marquess of Kendal. It is indeed a pleasure, Miss Standish." As he said her name, he finally caught her gaze.

Lord Ian scoffed. "But, my lord, no one has properly introduced you. Do you think you will be able to weather the scandal?"

Jes tilted her head to one side. Lord Kendal and Lord Ian sounded very similar except for a few subtle differences which would be difficult to detect when they were not together. But when in the same place, it was more obvious. Lord Kendal's speech was more refined and there was a sense of authority in his tone. She nodded at him. "You were here in the first week—on the house tour and the ghost hunt." Her voice quieted. "In the library."

Lord Kendal nodded his head, but still, he would not hold eye contact with her.

She turned to Lord Ian. "Have you both been here the entire time? The castle tour is the first time I am sure it was you." She turned back to Lord Kendal. "But you were here then, also."

"I arrived while everyone was attending church, before the excursion to the castle." Lord Ian smiled at her, but it was forced and false.

Now that she was really looking at them side by side, she could see other differences. The straightness of Lord Kendal's posture or even the slight quirk of Lord Ian's lip. As she looked closer she could see Lord Ian's nose was slightly crooked, as if it had been broken at some time. How had she not noticed this before?

She folded her arms across her chest, a scrutinizing gaze leveled at both men. Looking into the gentleman's eyes should have told her everything. Although, Lord Ian had not given her many chances to see his, except for the time in the hallway.

She turned her gaze to Lord Ian. "And you have been here ever since." She looked to Lord Kendal. "Where have you been of late? Did you quit the house altogether?"

Conrad shuffled from foot to foot. "My sister's condition worsened and I was summoned home."

As with the other times she had spoken with Lord Ia...Kendal, there was sincerity in his look.

Lord Ian interjected. "I was just telling my brother, there was no need for him to return. We are getting on famously without him."

Lord Kendal grunted. "I heard a different story, Ian. Now, do you not have a horse to win back or some such?" He made a shooing motion with his hands.

He turned to face her and for the first time since she walked in the room, he really looked at her. The air seemed thicker, harder to breathe. His voice dropped to a near whisper. "Now if you will excuse us, I have an important matter to discuss with Miss Standish." Lord Kendal spoke to his brother, but his intense gaze never left her face.

Jes could not stop wondering how she had missed these differences. Looking at them now, they did not seem so subtle. The longer she stood here, the more dimwitted she felt.

Lord Ian stomped his foot like a petulant child. "I will do no such thing. I have every right to stay. After all, I was the one invited. You were the pretender here, not me."

Jes felt Lord Kendal's breath on her neck as he sighed. He looked over to his brother. "It was not because I desired your life, I can assure you on that point."

Jes could see his anger rising toward Lord Ian. She could see Lord Kendal's pulse beating rapidly in his neck. But by all other outward appearances, he was in total control—another difference between the two men.

She took a step away from them as they continued to argue. Lord Ian contending she had great affection for him and Lord Kendal disputing the claim.

As she listened, her own anger built up inside until she could hold it in no longer. How dare they presume to know her mind and make decisions for her? Neither man, for at this moment she was not sure either of them was a gentleman, had earned the right to court her, let alone determine her future.

She snapped. "I am not a horse at Tattersall's for you to dicker and banter over." She felt her throat tighten, making it difficult to swallow. Her eyes began to blur and she knew within moments tears would begin to fall. It was a mortification she would not allow them to witness. Drawing herself up to her full height, she raised her chin and looked from one to the other. "You know what I think? I think you are a pair of jackanapes and I want nothing to do with the lot of you. Good day, *gentlemen*." The last word was spoken with sarcasm and disdain.

Turning on her heel, she walked quickly towards the door, barely registering the sound of her name as it echoed through the room. She rounded the door frame into the hallway, then picking up her skirts, she raced down the corridor to find her mother.

17

FORGIVENESS AND BALLS

*I*t seemed Conrad was destined to search endlessly for those he wished to find. First, it was Ian and now Jes. She had been scarce since their encounter yesterday. The Countess had introduced him to the party before dinner the previous night. Lady Rachel had been present, but Jes had chosen to take her meal in her chambers. Lady Rachel quirked a brow at him when the introduction was made but said nothing apart from the usual pleasantries.

Jes was not at breakfast either. He had checked every room he could think of to find her today, but it was all for naught. She was as elusive as the ghost on the third floor. It made his chest ache to think she wanted nothing to do with him, but he could understand. He deserved nothing less.

It was ironic, actually. He had finally found an intriguing, intelligent and witty woman to spend the rest of his life with and it seemed possible she would never have him. The Fates must be having their fun.

Conrad ducked into a small sitting room and found it empty.

He moved to the chair by the low-lying fire and slumped down, dropping his head into his hands. What a muddle this was. He leaned back, resting his head on the seat back of the chair, staring at the ceiling. An intricate plaster of vines looped around the perimeter of the room. Other thinner shoots moved towards the center of the room with leaves and blue flowers spread around the outer edges. It was not something he usually took note of, or rather, he had not until he toured the house with Jes. They had named this the Blue Flower and Vine Room. He had no idea what the actual name was. It would have required him to pay attention to Miss Graystock while she had given the tour, which he had not.

Taking a deep breath, Conrad focused on one flower, admiring the deep navy blue as it faded to an almost violet on the outer edges of the petals. A vibrant orange center accentuated the navy next to it. His lids felt heavy, his lack of sleep catching up to him. Thinking he would just shut his eyes for a moment, he slipped into the darkness of sleep.

"Excuse me, my lord." The request trudged through the heavy slumber, his mind too thick to process. "My lord, an urgent message has come for you."

A hand gave him a quick shove in the shoulder, bringing him out of his sleep. He squinted around the slightly darker room. The early morning sun must have moved higher in the sky, for it was no longer shining directly into the windows.

His focus settled on the footman standing before him. He rubbed a hand over his face. "What did you say?"

"Lord Kendal? A message was just delivered—one of your riders. He said it was urgent,"

Conrad nodded as he took the folded parchment, holding it close to his face until his eyes cleared. He stared at the wax seal, it finally waking him up fully. "Thank you, er Damen, is it?"

"Yes, my lord." It sounded as if there was a note of disdain in his voice, but Conrad shook it off. His stomach twisted. He was not sure if he wanted to know what was in this letter. Although, Jes already believed the worst. This letter would not bring any more pain, if it did, indeed, confirm what she believed.

Conrad broke the seal and read the letter through quickly, then a second time. A small smile curved his lips. Regardless of how things ended with her, he was glad he could do this for her and her mother.

He stood up, stretching his kinked body. He had to find her. This information could not wait any longer. Then, if she would not have him, he would leave. In time the ache in his chest would go away and he could look at a map without feeling... what? Joy followed closely by remorse. His shoulders dropped a fraction.

Tucking the parchment into the cuff of his sleeve, he moved out of the sitting room. Once in the hallway, he looked back and forth, trying to determine where to begin his search. This house was so large, he was not sure he would be able to locate her before they would need to begin readying for the ball.

Walking up and down the hallways, he poked his head in every room, making a quick perusal before continuing on to the next. He glanced into the ballroom, the opulence drawing him in. One of the maids spotted him and came over.

"May I help you find something, my lord?"

He hesitated. "I was wondering if anyone has seen Miss Standish of late. A letter was delivered for her." While technically not true, the contents of the letter were undoubtedly for her.

The girl shook her head. "I can ask the others, see if anyone has seen her."

Conrad nodded and the maid scurried over to a group of maids in the far corner of the room. He scrubbed a hand over his face, wiping the last remnants of the sleep from his eyes. His neck warmed when he noticed the eyes of all the servants in the hall looking at him. Several of the maids nodded their heads.

The maid returned. "Sarah and Fanny saw her walking to the third floor, my lord. The nursery wing."

Of course. He should have thought to look there. Jes seemed to have a curiosity about that wing. He offered the girl a brief bow. "Thank you very much. I shall continue my search there."

Stepping onto the landing of the third floor, he spotted the entrance to the nursery. A smile curved at his lips as he remembered the gooseflesh which had dotted Miss Standish's neck when they had seen the specter there—was it only last week? Conrad took a deep breath. How had he fallen completely in love with a woman in only a week?

He grasped his hands behind his back, walking slowly down the corridor, unable to find the mark on the runner where the candle had fallen. This entire house was full of memories.

He had not yet reached the halfway point of the corridor when a sound reached his ears. It took only a moment for him to recognize the screeching coming from a room across the hall. A smile curved his lips. It was the same song from the night of the musical, although it sounded even worse today. Jerky, stilted words making the singing more out of tune. Reaching the door, he realized it was crying causing the uneven sound. His heart sank to his toes. He rested his head against the door, his palm flat on the wood. Was he the cause of this?

He took several steps back, one fist clenched at his side as the other hand rubbed at his chest. It did nothing to relieve the pain. He wanted to speak to her—explain why he had not told her who he was from the beginning. Tell her he loved her. But maybe he needed to quit thinking about what he needed and think about what she needed for a change. He wished she needed him.

The letter crinkled in his shirtsleeve and he looked down at the parchment. This was what she needed now. Pushing off the wall, he moved to the door and knocked.

The singing stopped immediately, but the barrier between them remained. There were a few more sniffles, and then the door cracked open. Their eyes locked, hers widening before she closed the door.

"I would prefer not to be disturbed, Lord Kendal."

Joy at hearing his actual name from her lips battled with the disappointment of the door which stood between them. "I am sorry. I did not mean to intrude..." He stared at the wood. "I have something for you—a letter I thought you would be interested in reading. It concerns your father." He stood in place a moment longer, waiting to see if she would come out. When she did not appear, he stooped down to push the missive under the door. "When I discovered the First Lord of the Admiralty was attending a house party near Penymoor, it felt like providence." Before it was fully under, the door opened. Conrad pulled the letter to him and took a large step back.

Several tendrils of hair had escaped her pins and now hung down the side of her face. His breath sucked in. There was a smudge of something running up her left cheekbone. She had never looked more beautiful. The sparkle of freshly shed tears in her eyes caused him to swallow hard.

Her gaze flicked from his eyes to a spot somewhere down the corridor.

"You said there is a letter about my father?" She stood in front of the door with her hand hovering over the knob.

Conrad cleared his throat. "Oh, um. Yes." His head bobbed up and down foolishly. Glancing into the small room, he spotted a canvas in the corner, mostly obscured by shadows. Only the silhouette of a man was visible. Before he could get a good look the door slammed closed behind her.

He looked at Jes, a brow raised in question. "I did not know you painted." His head inclined toward the closed door.

"Just because I cannot sing does not mean I have no talents at all," she snapped. She pressed her lips tightly together before she spoke again. This time her voice was quiet and calm. "There are many things you do not know about me. Now, the letter, my lord?"

Conrad visibly flinched at the cut. He fingered the smooth paper, trying to gain some comfort from it before he gave it up. He lifted his hand, this time lightly touching her face and rubbing at the paint streak with his thumb.

She shuddered under his touch and seemed to lean into him. Her eyes closed for a moment before they opened wide and she took a step back.

"The letter." Her voice trembled as she held out her hand.

Conrad placed the folded square into her palm, then bowed. "There is so much I need to say..."

She took a step back into the room, closing the door on him.

He stared at the door. "I realize it is a false hope, but I would be honored if you saved one dance for me, Jes." He turned and walked down the corridor. Taking the stairs two at a time, he reached the bottom and made his escape to the stables.

———

JES CLUTCHED the letter in her hand, folding her arms across her middle to stop the roiling in her stomach. She leaned back against the door, closing her eyes. He had called her by her Christian name and she had never heard anything so lovely. Touching her cheek, she could still feel the heat radiating there.

Pushing back the curtains, the room filled with sunlight. She placed the parchment in her lap as she shook out her trembling hands. Examining the letter, she saw Lord Kendal's name scrawled across the front. Why would he give her one of his personal letters? She did not recognize the wax seal. Slowly unfolding the paper, she started at the top and began to read. Her breath came in frenzied bursts as the words began to swim in her eyes. Could this be true?

Bursting from the closet room, Jes ran down the stairs to her mother's chambers. She did not knock or wait for her mother to admit her, but flung open the door, looking wildly about.

"Mama! Are you here?"

Her mother emerged from the small adjoining sitting room. "Jes, good heavens, dearest. What is the matter?"

Jes thrust the letter into her mother's hands.

"What is this?" Her mother read the opening salutation, her eyebrows raising as she looked at her daughter. "Why do you have a letter for Lord Kendal?"

Jes danced from foot to foot, shaking her head in agitation. "He found me and gave it to me, but that is not the point, Mama. Read it."

Lady Rachel moved to the chair by the window and picked up a small pair of glasses. She gave Jes one last questioning look before turning her attention to the letter.

Jes sat on the edge of the bed, wringing her hands as she watched her mother read painfully slow. She heard her mother's intake of breath, saw as her hands began to shake.

Lady Rachel looked up. "Is this true? What did Lord Kendal say?"

Jes shook her head. "He said nothing about the letter." Jes stood up and paced the floor by the bed. "Oh, I do not remember his exact words, something about someone being at a house party nearby. He found me while I was singing and painting and..." Jes grimaced, "crying. Over him no less! But Mama, if the letter is true, this changes everything for us."

Her mother began reading the letter aloud. "'I was surprised by your inquiry concerning the fleet of Mr. James Standish. Your information about Mr. Standish's demise is correct, however, upon further investigation, it seems you have been misinformed about the other two ships. While both the *Eye of India* and the *Cleopatra* sustained severe damage, they entered Hull with their cargo intact.'" Lady Rachel stared at the letter, her brow furrowed, her head shaking lightly. Finally, she looked up, catching Jes's gaze. "We have already paid the creditors for the goods on those ships. It will not make us wealthy, but once it is all sold, I believe we could live quite comfortably. We shall not be required to live on your cousin's generosity. I could once again provide you with a dowry. While it will not be as substantial, it will be respectable."

Jes nodded as tears once again began to stream down her face. "Will we still live at Morley Park? We could live somewhere else."

"If the offer of the dower house still stands, I believe I should very much like to live at Morley." Lady Rachel sat silently staring at the paper, her head shaking in wonderment. Then a smile curved her lips. "This letter does have other ramifications."

Jes studied her mother, her forehead pulled down in question.

"A gentleman does not go to the trouble or call in favors from the First Lord of the Admiralty for someone he does not care for deeply. If this is not an act of love, I don't know what is."

Jes shook her head, unready to accept this new revelation. "I am sure it was just a guilty conscience which urged him to inquire. Nothing more."

Her mother tsked quietly before asking, "What did he do that was so bad? You have already figured out Lord Ian was the one responsible for all the reprehensible behavior."

"Mother. He lied, made a fool of me—of us all. And did you

not caution me about my regard for him after the waltz we shared?" Her voice ringed with challenge.

"Do not take that tone with me, young lady." Lady Rachel frowned. "My warnings were when we thought his actions inconsistent. I was concerned his overtures were false or, at the very least, fleeting. We know the truth and I have no reservations. Lord Kendal always treated you with the utmost respect. He is not a liar, my dear."

"Of course he is!" How could her mother take his side after all he had done?

"Did he introduce himself as Lord Ian?" Her mother asked.

Jes thought back to their encounter in the parlor before dinner on that first night. "No. I approached him and reminded him of our acquaintance in London."

Her mother smiled smugly. "Precisely."

Jes glowered. "Omission is just as much a lie, Mama. You have told me so on several occasions."

Lady Rachel's tone gentled and she beckoned her daughter to come to her.

Jes kneeled on the floor in front of her mother, looking up into her face. Fingering a lock of hair, Lady Rachel tucked it behind Jes's ear. "Give him a chance, dearest. He loves you. I can see it in his eyes. I believe he is a good man who will love you as your father loved me. Let him explain himself. Don't give up a chance at love because of pride."

Jes pulled her hands away and looked at them, her heart and mind warring within her. "I don't know, Mama." She bit the inside of her lip. "It may be too late, anyhow. I spoke terribly to him. Especially in light of all he has done for us." She looked at the letter sitting on her mother's lap.

Lady Rachel stood up, helping Jes to her feet. She held up the parchment. "When a gentleman goes to this much trouble, a few terse words will not deter him, I assure you. Now, it is time to get ready for the ball. I think tonight you should look especially handsome." Her mother went to her wardrobe and pulled out the beautiful lilac ball gown with a black lace overlay. It was breathtaking.

"Oh, Mama," Jes breathed out.

Lady Rachel smiled. "I wanted it to be a surprise."

JES ENTERED the Marble Ballroom and gaped. She had thought the room pretty on the house tour, but now flower arrangements dotted the corners and the crystals shimmered with candlelight.

She adjusted her long gloves, feeling as beautiful as her surroundings, for once. She scanned the faces of those already gathered, trying to find one person specifically. Her breath caught as she saw him in the far corner, speaking with Lady Summers. Stomach sinking panic set in when he fingered a ringlet by the lady's ear.

He turned in her direction, and all of the air whooshed out of her. It was not Conrad. *Conrad*, she whispered to herself. Oh, how she liked the sound of his name.

Lord Ian caught her gaze and winked as he ran his finger along Lady Summer's cheekbone.

Jes looked away, embarrassed for the both of them.

She continued to examine everyone, as she tried to find Conrad. Her mother was right. She needed to hear his explanation. What if he had left already? She had told him she did not wish to see him again. Why would he stay? Desperation nearly swallowed her. How had she ruined everything so thoroughly?

The orchestra began to tune their instruments and a low buzzing floated through the air as people sought their partners.

Jes saw Lord Bloomsbury walking in her direction. Her eyes

widened and a sinking feeling twisted her stomach as he approached.

"Miss Standish, may I claim the first dance?" His head was already dotted with perspiration and his hair was beginning to slide forward. If the first dance was a reel, it would surely slide the rest the way forward. Whoever was his partner would receive a perspiration shower when he flung it back into place. Jes prayed it was not a cotillion. She did not think she could stand up with Bloomsbury for that lengthy of a dance.

Her face puckered in distaste. Although, perhaps it would be better to dance with him before he was fully drenched in sweat.

Jes curtsied and put a false smile on her face. "I am honored you have singled me out, my lord." She thought he had turned his attentions elsewhere. Placing her hand on his arm, she allowed him to lead her to the dance floor. Standing as far away from him as possible while still being part of the line, she touched him only when required and kept her eyes searching the ballroom for latecomers.

Finally, the music ended and she was able to curtsy and make her escape, having narrowly missed his hair spray on two occasions. Jes moved to the side, her anxiety building. A breeze blew in from one of the open terrace doors. No longer caring to watch the dancing, Jes made her way through the crowd. Once outside, she took in a deep breath, placing her elbows on the thick stone railing. She leaned her head forward, massaging her temple with her fingers.

"May I claim your waltz? I happen to know we are very well suited for that dance."

Still staring out into the gardens, Jes let Conrad's voice wash over her. "I believe the last time we waltzed, you made a hasty retreat back to Penymoor." He had come; she wanted to shout out loud.

"If I promise to never leave you again, will you say yes?" His voice was tentative and hopeful.

A smile twitched at the corner of her mouth. "Well, I did just dance with Lord Bloomsbury. Do you think you can match his...enthusiasm?"

His deep chuckle sounded behind her, raising the gooseflesh on her arms. She was grateful for the railing which was currently holding her up.

He moved closer, the heat from his body warming the air around her. "Jes, how could anyone partnered with you not show great enthusiasm? I believe your nature brings it out in others."

She closed her eyes when he said her name. Then opening them once more, she straightened her spine and took a deep breath. "Why did you lie? Why the charade of being your brother?"

Jes heard him run his hand through his hair. "It started out as a harmless way to give Ian a little more time at another house party. The dates overlapped and he was concerned if he arrived late, it would offend the Countess. She is one of the few matrons who still thinks him charming." He came to stand next to her, placing his elbows on the railing.

Jes glanced at him from the corner of her eye. He was staring straight ahead.

"He promised if I came and pretended to be him until he arrived, he would make an offer to Miss Simmons and settle down. I hoped he was in earnest. Ian is in need of...a calming influence. I believed this young lady would provide it. His life has been spinning out of control of late. If my doing this small thing would put him back on course, I was willing to make the sacrifice."

Jes felt him turn his gaze on her.

"It was only to be for a few days, and I did not believe I would encounter anyone who would capture my attention so completely." He turned and looked at her. "By the time I realized—well it was too late. I thought about pretending to come as myself, once Ian showed up, but by then you were friends with Lord Ian, not Lord Kendal." He sighed heavily. "I was afraid you would never speak to me again. If I could take it back I would."

"All of it?" She needed to know if he regretted everything.

"No, only the original lie. I could never wish the rest had never happened. Even if you decide to never see me again."

Jes turned to face him. "Thank you." He opened his mouth to respond but she shook her head. "Please, let me finish. Thank you for giving me the letter." Her voice shook. "Thank you for inquiring on our behalf. I am sure you had to request a great many favors to get the information so quickly. You don't know what you have given my mother. While she would never admit to it, being reliant for support, upon first my aunt and then my cousin, was hard for her. From what I have been told, my grandfather was a very proud man. I am afraid both my mother and I have inherited that trait from him." She breathed in again as emotion started to overtake her. "Because of you, we can stay on at Morley Park without feeling like a burden."

"Shearsby has no such notions about you and your mother. When I happened upon him on my way back to Penymoor, he could say nothing but kind things about you both. He was quite relieved to learn of your whereabouts." Jes smiled as another puzzle piece fell into place. She opened her mouth to reply, but he put his finger to her lips. They felt chilled when he lowered his hand. "While I respect your mother a great deal, I did it for you. That day in the library—how could I not use every resource I have to help you?"

His voice dropped so low, she had to lean closer to hear him. "I would do anything for you—for your happiness. If you still wish me to leave, I will depart this very moment."

Jes reached out and grasped his arm, shaking her head vigorously. "No. I do not wish that. I am sorry for what I said to you yesterday. I let my pride get the better of me."

He raised a hand to her cheek. "You need not apologize for anything." His heart felt like it might burst with happiness. There was only one thing which remained. "I love you, Jes. I want you to be my wife, as soon as possible." He paused. "Will you marry me?"

She leaned into the warmth, feeling everything in her world righting itself. "Of course, I will marry you. Can you truly wonder at my affections?"

He pulled back slightly, raising a brow. "Not anymore. But I should like to hear it all the same."

"I love you Conrad Pinkerton, Marquess of Kendal." It came out breathless and almost reverent.

Conrad's smile stretched from ear to ear. "I believe I hear the first strains of the waltz in the Checkerboard Room. Shall we, my love?"

Jes had thought the sound of her name on his lips was beautiful, but hearing him call her 'my love' was more perfect than anything she had ever heard before.

18

PORTRAITS AND KISSES

onrad's cheeks hurt from smiling. He must have smiled even while he slept because the pinch in his face was still present when he awoke.

As he walked into the breakfast room, his step lightened and his stomach pitched in anticipation of seeing Jes. His hopes sank when he looked about and found her noticeably absent. He grumbled under his breath as he turned and left the room.

Where could she be? There was little time left before the carriages would be called up and she would move on to Morley Park. Conrad checked the library and found it empty. He snapped his fingers as the image of her little painting room entered his mind.

Taking the stairs two at a time, he found himself outside of the storage room. The door stood slightly ajar, a quiet humming coming from inside. Conrad quirked a brow. The sound was not unpleasant. Curious.

He put a hand to the door and pushed it open even farther. The curtain at the window was pushed all the way to the side, flooding the room with light. Jes sat on a small stool in front of a large canvas, bathed in the same sunshine. The image took his breath away.

He stepped inside just as Jes looked up, a smile crinkling the corners of her eyes when she saw him. Ripples of excitement started in his toes and moved throughout his body. How had he not realized sooner how much he loved this woman?

She stood up, tension hovering around her. "Good morning, my lord."

Conrad growled, taking a step closer. "We are to be my lording, today, Miss Standish? I thought we were past all that."

The small frown turning down her lips brought a smile to his face. She did not like the formality any more than he did.

She looked up into his face. "I was only making sure last night was not a dream." Her voice was quiet.

Conrad reached out and grasped her hand in his. Rubbing his thumb over her knuckles, he slowly shook his head. "Although it would have been a most incredible dream, I can assure you, *Jes*, it is our reality. Which makes it all the better."

"And what does reality hold for us today?" She stood tall with her head high, but he could hear a touch of disappointment in her voice.

"I believe you and your mother are destined for Morley Park, are you not?"

Jes nodded her head. "And where are you destined for, Conrad?"

He smiled at her use of his Christian name and took her other hand in his. "I thought we discussed this last night. I am for London. I have an appointment with the Archbishop."

He closed the distance between them, her skirt swishing against his legs. Raising a hand to her cheek, he felt his chest warm as she leaned into it, placing her own hand over his.

"Jes." Her name came out on a whisper. He put his other hand on her waist, mostly sure she would not back away. Pulses of tingling heat shot through him when she moved her body closer to him and her eyes fluttered shut. He dropped his head as she raised hers, meeting somewhere in the middle. His lips brushed against hers, tentative at first. But then something exploded within him and he could not pull her close enough. He felt their heartbeats racing in unison.

Moving his hand from her cheek to the back of her neck, his thumb rubbed lightly back and forth along the slope of her neck and shoulder. He sprinkled a fluttering of kisses along her cheekbone—ending at her earlobe. His mind felt foggy, unable to think. His only thought was he wanted her to himself. The idea startled him. And he backed up a step. Then several more. He needed to put some distance between them or—he did not want to think about what he wanted. At least not yet.

He was still close enough to reach out and wind a loose tendril of hair around his finger. The curl stretched as she pulled back from him.

Determination glittered in her eyes and she set about gathering up her brushes, putting them in a pile on a canvas cloth on the nearby table. "Must you depart for London today?"

Conrad sighed. "You know why I am going to London, Jes. I need to procure a special license. I want us to marry as soon as possible."

She looked up from her brushes, an adorable pout on her lips. "But it will only shorten the time by a week, at most. I would rather we be together for three short weeks than apart for one long week."

His heart melted, which he guessed was part of her plan. He suspected she knew the effect she was having on him. "But we could be married in two weeks." He reached for her hand, pulling her to him. Sliding his arms around her waist, he pulled her up against him. "Perhaps a compromise? I would enjoy London all the more if I was accompanied by a lovely young lady and her mother."

She stepped out of his arms. Putting her hands on his shoulders, she pushed him back until there was space between them. "I have a difficult time thinking when you stand so close."

"Yes, I know the feeling." Conrad waggled his brows at her. He stepped toward her, but she stepped back. They preceded this way for several steps until she was backed into the corner.

He placed a hand on the walls on either side of her shoulders. "Will you accompany me to London, Jes?" Her smile grew. Life with this woman would never be dull, of that he was certain.

She ducked under his arm quicker than he could catch her. Dancing to the far wall, she turned around, laughter bubbling in her voice. "I thought you wished to ask my cousin for his consent? What if he withholds it after we have gone all the way to London?"

"He will not. I can assure you of that. Shearsby is one of my closest friends. He will be overjoyed."

Her lips twitched slightly, but her countenance displayed a touch of doubt.

Conrad faltered. "Perhaps not overjoyed. But he will not withhold his consent." When she did not look convinced, he moved closer. "Truly, you believe he would think me unworthy of you?" His brow furrowed. He shrugged a shoulder in defeat. "He would be correct, considering my actions of the last few weeks." His plans no longer seemed guaranteed. "What if he does not approve?"

She snorted as laughter erupted. Her eyes grew wide and her hand flew to cover her mouth.

Conrad could not help his own chuckle and he wrapped his arms around her waist.

She intertwined her fingers at the back of his neck. "I know my cousin, Conrad. If I am happy, he will be happy. There is no need to worry."

Conrad dipped his head, resting his brow against hers. "And are you happy, my love?"

"Very much so."

SOMEONE CLEARED a throat from the doorway.

Jes jumped back, nearly pulling Conrad with her as they tried to disentangle themselves. She felt her face heat when she saw her mother standing there, a knowing look on her face.

They had not been caught doing anything so very untoward. But moments ago...? Thanks to Jes's blushing, there was very little for her mother to guess on.

Conrad cleared his throat and Jes returned her gaze to him. Her heart flip-flopped. Then he smiled and her knees went weak. Would he always elicit this reaction?

"Lady Rachel." There was joy, but no guilt evident in his tone. "How are you this fine morning?"

She turned her shrewd gaze to him. "Very well, Lord Kendal." Her eyes flicked between them. "I hope I did not interrupt anything."

Conrad grinned, a bit wickedly in Jes's opinion. Ah! Now her mother surely knew.

Lady Rachel shook her head, an exasperated sigh pushing through her lips. "At least the door was open," she muttered.

Jes looked with wide eyes at Conrad over her mother's head. She had forgotten the door had been open. What if a maid had seen them?

Conrad continued to smile. He stepped around her mother and came to stand beside Jes. Retaking her hand in his, he laced his fingers through hers then turned to Lady Rachel. "I was asking Jes if the two of you would do me the honor of accompanying me to London. I have a matter of business..." He looked over at Jes and the love she saw there made her forget everything else. How had such a man fallen in love with her? She felt a bit jealous when he pulled his eyes away from her and looked again to her mother.

Jes wanted to reach up and bring his gaze back, but she refrained. Instead, she placed her hand high on his arm, squeezing his tight muscle. The pink tint which came into his earlobes told her he was affected as much as she.

"My business should only take a day or two at most. Then I can escort the both of you to Morley Park. There is something I wish to discuss with His Grace."

Lady Rachel looked as if she was trying to hold back a laugh. "I shall pen a note to my nephew and inform him of our delay." She headed to the doorway, where she stopped and turned back. "Thank you, Lord Kendal."

Conrad looked perplexed. "For what, my lady?"

"Surely you must know how grateful we are for the information you obtained about my late husband's ships."

Conrad waved her away. "The right people happened to be at the right place at the right time. That is all. I am just glad I could be of service, my..."

"But there is more," she cut him off. "I have always thought my Jes beautiful, but she has never shined as she does with you. You make her laugh, something which has been absent for too long." Lady Rachel smiled through glistening eyes. "Thank you for giving me my daughter back."

Before she could cross the threshold, Conrad stepped forward. "I love her, my lady."

She turned again, her head nodding. "I know." Then she stepped into the hallway and disappeared.

Jes stood still, her throat tight with emotion.

He came behind her. Sliding his arms around her waist, he pulled her against him, resting his chin on her head. The canvas lay in front of them. "You have been painting Shearsby?"

Jes nodded "He has yet to sit for his portrait. I thought I could present it to him as a gift when we arrive, to thank him for allowing us to live at Morley. Neither my grandfather nor my uncle would have allowed us to visit, much less live at the estate."

"It is a lovely present. When I saw it yesterday, I was not able to discern who it was." Was that jealousy in his tone? Or was it something else? Jes cocked her head, looking at him from the corner of her eye. A sheepish look crossed his features.

Jes grinned, slightly bumping her shoulder into his chest. "You thought it was you, did you not?"

Conrad shrugged, even as his face deepened in color. "The room was dark, and I only saw the silhouette."

She turned in his arms, looking up. Grasping his chin between her thumb and forefinger, she turned his head to one side. "When a person is as handsome as you, it is hard to imagine why you were not the subject."

He turned his head quickly, brushing a kiss along her fingertips.

Rising up on her tiptoes, she brushed a quick kiss across his lips. "I plan to remedy the error as soon as possible, but only if it can hang in my personal sitting room."

He pressed a kiss to her forehead and then the tip of her nose. "Or we could hang it in the gallery with all the other portraits and you can just keep me in your personal sitting room." His brow waggled.

Jes ran a finger over his jaw. "Yes, that is a much better plan." She leaned up, pressing her lips to his for one last kiss, thrilled to know there would be more of them to come.

EPILOGUE

Welcome Home

*J*es stared out the window of the carriage as it rolled up the drive towards Penymoor. Her mouth dropped open as the carriage rounded the bend and the expansive home appeared.

"Welcome home, my love," Conrad whispered in her ear before placing a kiss on her neck.

A quiet giggle sounded from across the carriage. Jes lifted her eyes and smiled at Conrad's sister, Jane. He winked and she giggled again.

"Oh, Conrad. It is beautiful." She sat back on the bench, but her gaze still stayed focused on the view outside.

He wrapped his arms around her waist, pulling her closer to his side. "It will be even lovelier having you here. I can scarcely remember how I existed here without you."

Jes grinned up at him. "And they say Ian is the charming one. I will never understand that."

Conrad stared down at her. "Let's not talk about Ian, shall we?"

The carriage came to a stop and the door opened. Conrad stepped down and waited for her to emerge. When she stepped out, the sight of the servants lining the entry stairs caused her breath to hitch in her throat. Never in her wildest dreams had she imagined herself in this situation. She had always dreamed of marrying for love and the man in her dreams looked just like her husband, with a few exceptions. But living in and being mistress of a grand estate had never been a part of the dream. Their town-home in Hartlepool was the best to be had in that seaside town, but it did not even compare to this.

Conrad helped Jane and Miss Partridge from the carriage but then recaptured Jes's hand, placing it on his arm. As they began to walk towards the butler, he placed his hand on the top of hers.

"Frampton, Mrs. Bender, I would like to introduce you to my wife. Lady Kendal."

The butler bowed and the housekeeper curtsied. Then all of the staff followed suit as she walked with Conrad up the front steps. Frampton proceded them to the front door and opened it wide as they approached.

Jane ripped off her bonnet and gloves. She tossed them at Frampton as she half walked half ran inside while Miss Partridge hurried to catch up.

Jes smiled after the energetic girl. Although they had only met a few days earlier, Jes already loved her as a sister. She would miss Jane while they went on their wedding tour.

Conrad guided Jes inside. She stopped in the entryway and stared at the two set of stairs going up on either side. A large, glittering chandelier hung down in the center of the room. Frampton stood beside them, taking Conrad's beaver and gloves.

Frampton stood still as Jes turned in a circle, taking everything in. She stopped when Conrad chuckled at her side. Quirking a brow at him she asked, "What do you find so amusing, my lord?"

Conrad pouted. "My lord? What happened to my love? I liked it much better."

Her face heated and she glanced at Frampton. The man kept his eyes averted, though she thought she noticed a twinkle.

Putting his finger to her chin, Conrad turned her face back to him. "Frampton does not mind if you call me my love. I believe he will enjoy the respite from hearing me curse."

Frampton stood stoically. "You are correct, my lord."

Chuckling, Conrad pulled the ribbons of her bonnet, releasing the bow under her chin. He took the hat off and handed it to the butler. Jes worked the fingers of her gloves, pulling them off and handing them to him also.

The butler bowed and disappeared down the hallway.

Conrad grabbed Jes around the waist, and lifting her feet off the ground, he spun her around. "Jes, my love, we are home."

She squealed with laughter until he set her down. "And what shall we do now?" He bent towards her, his gaze bouncing from her eyes to her lips.

Jes pulled away. "Perhaps a tour?"

CONRAD GROWLED. "That was not what I had in mind." He grabbed her hand and laced their fingers together, guiding her into the first room off the entryway—a sitting room. It was painted a pale green with white wainscoting and chair rail. The ceiling was coved with a fresco mural clearly the main attraction of the room. Greek gods and goddesses draped in white toga sat eating grapes and drinking wine.

Her eyes widened as she took it all in. "What is this room called?"

Conrad looked around. It had been called the Fresco Sitting room his entire life. Perhaps it was time for a change. "What do you think we should call it?"

Jes smiled. "The Green Toga room?"

Conrad laughed as he nodded. "Yes. That is a much better name." He pointed to the cluster of chairs in the corner, a tingle of joy working in his stomach. "Did you know, Lord Byron and Lord Wellington planned the battle of Trafalgar, right in that very corner?"

Jes grinned up at him.

He bent and placed a kiss on her nose. "There are many great things I will teach you about this house."

She put her arms around him and laid her head on his chest. "I can barely contain my excitement." Pulling back, she raised her pert brow at him. "But those stories can wait. For now, where did you say my personal sitting room is?"

Conrad stooped down and swished her up into his arms, holding her tight against him. "Right this way, my love."

19

SNEAK PEEK OF REFORMING THE GAMBLER

*L*ord Ian Pinkerton steered his horse onto the graveled drive, letting the breeze blow the tension from his shoulders. His life was about to return to normal and by end of month, he would be back in London enjoying the pleasures it had to offer someone of his station. Winning this estate a fortnight ago was what he'd needed.

At present, except for the clothes in his trunk, this estate was his only possession. Even his horse wasn't his own.

Ian's shoulders tightened, pain shooting up the back of his neck, making his head throb. Conrad—His Greatness, the Marquess of Kendal and Ian's identical twin—was never at a loss for words where Ian was concerned. Conrad had not even given Ian the papers of ownership for the horse he was riding. He had said the animal could not be gambled away without them.

Ian smirked. Nobody cared about papers when in the throws of a good wager. Ian's hold tightened on the reins, causing Ethelred to toss his head several times.

"If," Conrad had said, "you do manage to lose Ethelred on a bet, I will have you hanged for horse thievery."

Ian shifted in his saddle. He didn't believe Conrad would actually follow through on the threat, but Ian hadn't believed his brother would cut him off financially, either.

Ian growled low in his throat. His Greatness thought himself so above everyone.

Shaking out his arms and shoulders, Ian took several deep breaths and relaxed into his saddle. A tingle in his stomach accompanied the grin on his face. For now, this estate would provide the needed refuge from his creditors while he arranged for its sale. Then he would be flush. Perhaps there would be enough left over to increase his station.

Ian's breath hitched as Dunbarton came into view, only to whoosh from his lungs a moment later.

His mouth dropped open and he pulled Ethelred to a stop. This was it? This was his great winnings? He stooped forward, his head shaking slightly. The castle before him was grand, or it had been forty years prior. Now it looked to be almost in ruins.

Ian choked on a cry, tears stinging his eyes. Wesley had told him the house was in need of small repairs to ready it for sale...but this?

A large man ambled out of the small house to the side of the drive. He stopped when he saw Ian. In his prime, the man was likely taller than Ian, by at least a hand, but with his stooped back and shoulders he was surely an inch or two shorter.

"Can I help you, sir?" His gruff Scottish accent made it difficult to understand all of his words.

Ian slid from his horse, standing in front of the old man. "I am Lord Ian Pinkerton and this is my estate."

The man shook his head. "I am the bailiff here. And I know Mr. Charles Wesley is the owner of this estate."

Ian tipped his head to the side. If he left now, perhaps he could make it back to Westmorland by the end of day tomorrow next. He could try reasoning with Conrad again and forget this whole thing had ever happened. Why had he told Conrad he did not need him or his money? Would it be so difficult to live as his brother demanded?

Ian dropped his head back and looked up at the sky. There was also the matter of the house party he had planned. Why had he invited his friends to join him here? Ian chided himself. It was all to prove he was not as desperate as was actually the case.

He reached a hand into his saddlebag and withdrew a paper, handing it over to the old man. "This paper indicates Mr. Wesley lost this estate to me in a hand of whist." Ian turned his eyes back to the castle, muttering. "Although, his descriptions were vastly different from reality."

The man squinted at the paper, rubbing a hand over his bristled chin. "You said you were a lord?"

Ian nodded absently. "In name only. My father was the Marquess of Kendal. A title my brother now holds." Did the bailiff look disappointed? It was not the first time Ian had seen that look. What did Ian care what this stranger thought of him? He turned, looking at the missing windows and crumbling rock edifice. "And you are?"

"Mr. Docherty. I have been the bailiff of this estate for the past twenty years."

Ian gave the man a bland expression. "You may not wish to admit as much. The estate does not show you as...capable in your duties."

Mr. Docherty glared at Ian. "I cannot do what I have not been given funds for. If not for me, this house would be a pile of rubble. I have not received a pence in nearly a decade."

Ian's brow furrowed. "Why do you stay?"

"My family has worked at this castle for over three hundred years. They helped build it for the Chief of the MacDillon Clan in the late fourteen hundreds." He raised his chin, pride evident in his look. "I will stay until I am no longer allowed to remain."

Ian rubbed at his chest as it warmed. What made a man stay even though he received nothing for his work? Not even an acknowledgment or a word of thanks. It was odd, to say the least.

Docherty's eyes widened slightly. "Have you come to restore Dunbarton to its former grandeur?"

Ian began to run a hand through his hair but quickly pulled it back, instead fisting it at his side. Conrad always mussed his hair when he was frustrated. Ian cared too much about his appearance to do such a thing, but lately, he'd found himself doing it without thinking. "It was my intention, but..." His gaze drifted back to the large castle.

"Were you not told it was in need of repair?" The old man followed Ian's gaze.

"Repair? Wesley indicated the house was in need of *minor work*." Ian looked at the missing south side roof. The lump formed in his throat again and he rubbed at his temple with his fingers. "Is there any place not on the verge of collapsing? Or shall I return to the village and secure lodging there?"

The old man rubbed at the scruff on his chin. "The dower house is habitable. Most likely not up to your standards, but it will keep the rain off."

Ian sighed. "And where is this dower house?"

Docherty motioned with his head down the lane Ian had just traveled. "It is on the left, just as you enter the estate. It is set back a ways, so you may have missed it when you came in." He turned away from Ian. "I will inform the Mrs. of your arrival and have her see to the dust covers."

Nodding to no one, Ian placed his foot in the stirrup. "I would be grateful for her help. I believe I will return to Tobermory. I have a letter I need to post...immediately."

Docherty disappeared down a neatly trimmed path. As Ian looked around him, he could see the areas where money was not needed for upkeep. The hedges and trees were all cut and maintained. The gardens to the left, what Ian could see of them, appeared quite lovely.

Ian looked one last time at the castle and slumped in his saddle. His guests could not sleep in the gardens when they visited. He was still in a muddle, even if the grounds were well kept. His stomach burned and gurgled at the thought of asking Conrad for money. But he had few other options.

Tugging the reins to the right, Ian directed his horse back down the lane toward the village. His throat was dry and he felt like his mouth was full of sand. He needed a drink.

As he spotted the dower house, he pulled his horse to a stop. He could determine the outline of the cottage, for that was the best description. It was barely visible behind a copse of trees. Seeing how well the rest of the grounds were kept, Ian could only assume the house was intentionally hidden. Ian glared at the trees, his teeth grinding together. *When I find Wesley...* A facer was the least that scoundrel deserved.

Turning from the drive, he continued on to Tobermory. He felt the pocket where his watch had once resided, but now only a few coins occupied the space. He did not have even enough funds to purchase parchment and ink, let alone frank the letter.

As he entered the village, he spotted an inn to the left. Feeling thirstier than he had in days, he veered in that direction, deciding his letter could wait.

Ian entered the darkened, mostly empty, tap room. Looking for the darkest corner, he sat down and dropped his head into his hands.

189

A skinny man wearing an apron came from a back room. "What can I get you, sir?"

Without thought, Ian murmured, "Whiskey."

The man bobbed his head and moved to a long bar top. Withdrawing a bottle from beneath, he poured some into a glass. Setting it on the table in front of Ian, the innkeeper asked, "You visiting Mull, sir?"

Ian shook his head, draining the glass in one swallow. "If only I were so fortunate. I am the new owner of Dunbarton." He tapped the glass.

The man picked it up. "The place was not as you expected?"

Ian shrugged. "I expected it to at least have a roof."

The innkeeper left, returning with a bottle in hand. He poured some more of the amber liquid into Ian's glass.

"And what be the name of the new master of Dunbarton?"

Ian again drained the glass. His empty stomach churned as the liquor settled. "Lord Ian Pinkerton."

The innkeeper bowed. "Welcome to Mull, my lord."

Ian grunted and tapped the glass again.

The innkeeper stared at Ian. "Will you be settling the bill today, my lord?"

Ian shook his head. "I have only just arrived and am short on coin. You can request payment from the Marquess of Kendal at Penymoor in Westmorland." A smile turned up the corners of Ian's mouth as he imagined Conrad's reaction when the request for payment arrived. The least his brother could do was pay for a few drinks. Ian looked at the man pointedly and tapped the glass again, harder this time.

The innkeeper raised a brow. "Would you care for some food, my lord?"

Ian shook his head before closing his eyes and dropping his head back into his hands. He needed to write to Conrad, but he couldn't bring himself to leave the table. Until recently, Conrad had always lectured Ian, pacing about the floor before finally relenting and giving Ian the money he sought. But since the house party last summer, Conrad had changed. Oh, he still lectured, but no blunt followed. Ian knew asking for his help was risky, but he did not see any other option. Conrad would likely demand the estate be put in his own name until Ian paid him back.

Ian sighed. He missed the old Conrad. His brother had not always been the serious, curmudgeon he was now. When they were children, he had been fun. A memory flitted to the surface of his mind.

Ian stood on the table in the schoolroom, his wooden sword above his head. "I claim this land for King Harold of the Britain's."

Conrad circled the table, fighting off several imaginary foes. As he dispatched the last unlucky man, he raised his sword, crossing it with Ian's. "Long live King Harold! Long live Britain!"

Nurse Eleanor entered the room, a soft smile on her face. "Lord Ian, please remove yourself from the tabletop."

Ian hopped off the table, slashing his sword through the air. "It is not a table, Nurse Eleanor. It is the last stronghold of our enemy, the evil Mordred. We have conquered him at last."

Nurse Eleanor chuckled. "Perhaps we should pick a different story to read tonight."

Conrad's eyes widened. "Oh, no. Please, let us continue the story of Arthur. Please."

Nurse Eleanor shook her head, but her eyes danced with laughter. "Very well, but please take your strong hold out of doors. Your sister needs to rest."

A throat cleared from the doorway. "Nurse Eleanor, I will be taking Lord Whitmore every day at this time, until he returns to Eton. He needs to begin his training."

Conrad sulked, his sword dropping to his side. "But father, Ian and I..."

His father raised a brow. It was the look which meant he would brook no more argument. "Ian may continue to play. I have no need of him right now. It will not take long to teach him what he will need to know to manage a small estate."

The innkeeper poured another glass; the swish of the liquid brought Ian's head up.

In the end, the training to run even a small estate was for naught. His mother had changed her mind and he had not inherited anything.

Ian picked up the glass. He would have one more drink and then he would write to his brother.

AFTERWORD

Dear Reader,

Thank you so much for reading! As the saying goes, I hope you laughed, and cried and that it stirred all emotions. That was the intention when I wrote it.

Somerstone was based on Wentworth Woodhouse Estate. All of the monuments, follies, obelisks, and rock formations are located on or around this great estate. Most are referred to as their actual names. Wentworth Castle is also an actual castle near Wentworth Woodhouse. The stories about the family feuds mentioned in the story are based on actual stories surrounding the house. The chapel everyone attended is based on the Old Holy Trinity Church in Yorkshire. Much of the history Conrad mentions to Jes about the church is based on Old Holy Trinity Church.

The ghost stories came from various sources. The Wentworth Castle ghost story is an actual story from Wentworth Castle (Lady

Lucy's walk). The Brown Lady ghost story is based on the Brown Lady of Raynham Hall in Norfolk. The ghost story of the young boy was based on the story of Sir George Sitwell of Reinshaw Hall.

This book was the result of a super fun and crazy experiment that turned out better than I could ever have imagined. Mistaken Identity is the third book in the Regency House Party: Somerstone series. There are more series in the works. The other books in the series are: The Unwanted Suitor, The Stable Master's Daughter, An Unlikely Courtship and Tabitha's Folly

Be sure to check out my other stories:
    An American in Duke's Clothing
    Reforming the Gambler

Happy reading!
    Mindy

ABOUT THE AUTHOR

Mindy loves all things history and romance, which makes reading and writing Regency romance right up her alley. When she isn't living in her alternate realities (she actually made an imaginary elevator in her closet when she was a kid), she is married to her real-life Mr. Darcy and trying to raise five proper boys (two of which are twins). They live happily in the beautiful mountains of Utah, where they enjoy camping, hiking and spending time together.

Made in the USA
Monee, IL
20 December 2020